BEAST

GALACTIC GLADIATORS #7

ANNA HACKETT

Beast

Published by Anna Hackett

Cover by Melody Simmons of eBookindiecovers

Edits by Tanya Saari

ISBN (ebook): 978-1-925539-35-6

ISBN (paperback): 978-1-925539-36-3

WHAT READERS ARE SAYING ABOUT ANNA'S ACTION ROMANCE

Unexplored – Romantic Book of the Year (Ruby) Novella Winner 2017

At Star's End – One of Library Journal's Best E-Original Romances for 2014

Return to Dark Earth – One of Library Journal's Best E-Original Books for 2015 and two-time SFR Galaxy Awards winner

The Phoenix Adventures – SFR Galaxy Award Winner for Most Fun New Series and "Why Isn't This a Movie?" Series

Beneath a Trojan Moon – SFR Galaxy Award Winner and RWAus Ella Award Winner

Hell Squad – Amazon Bestselling Science Fiction Romance Series and SFR Galaxy Award for best Post-Apocalypse for Readers who don't like Post-Apocalypse

The Anomaly Series – #1 Amazon Action Adventure Romance Bestseller

"Like Indiana Jones meets Star Wars. A treasure hunt with a steamy romance." – SFF Dragon, review of *Among Galactic Ruins*

"Strap in, enjoy the heat of romance and the daring of this group of space travellers!" – Di, Top 500 Amazon Reviewer, review of *At Star's End*

"Action, danger, aliens, romance – yup, it's another great book from Anna Hackett!" – Book Gannet Reviews, review of *Hell Squad: Marcus*

Sign up for my VIP mailing list and get your *free box set* containing three action-packed romances.

Visit here to get started:

www.annahackettbooks.com

CHAPTER ONE

An enraged roar woke her.

Mia Ross rolled, almost falling out of her bed. *Where was she?* It took her a second, scanning the shadowed room. *Bedroom. House of Galen. Planet of Carthago.*

Nowadays, it always took a moment for her to remember where she was when she first woke up. At least she wasn't in a cell.

Mia scrambled up and crossed to a chair. She grabbed the tangle of clothes, separating them. Being abducted off her supply ship from Earth by alien slavers probably accounted for the confusion. She pulled her trousers on, hopping on one foot. Being forced into an underground fight ring on a lawless desert planet, then rescued by alien gladiators, then snatched again by a crazy tech guru who wanted to use her for her brainpower, then rescued again, probably had a little to do with it as well.

She pulled her shirt over her head. No one could

blame a girl for waking up confused after everything she'd been through.

Another roar echoed through the hallway outside her room.

Mia raced out of her bedroom. It was the middle of the night, so the corridor was only lit by low lights set into the stone walls. As she hurried down the hallway, a door opened.

"Mia?"

She looked up and saw her friend and fellow human, Harper, standing in a doorway. "It's okay, Harper. I've got it. Go back to bed."

The former security specialist looked worried, her dark hair mussed by sleep. Suddenly, a big, tattooed gladiator appeared behind her.

"The guards can handle it, Mia," Raiden said.

A big, *naked*, tattooed alien gladiator. Mia averted her gaze, and was glad that Harper was blocking most of her man's body. The woman was one lucky lady. You didn't have to spend much time with Harper and Raiden to see that they were perfect for each other.

"No, I can calm him down," Mia said. "It'll be fine."

She hurried off before they tried to stop her. She jogged through the twists and turns of the House of Galen. The beautiful, warm stone walls were dotted with striking wall hangings made of red and gray fabric, all of them depicting gladiators fighting in the Kor Magna Arena.

Kor Magna was the largest city on the desert world of Carthago. It was famous for its gladiatorial arena, and for the human survivors from Fortuna Station, it was now home.

Reaching a set of stairs, she hurried down to the cells, giving her head an incredulous shake. God, her home was a gladiatorial house on an alien world. Earth and her life before felt very, very far away.

Her family would be equal parts horrified and curious. Mia smiled, a sweet pain piercing her chest. She missed them like crazy. She'd always been the odd one out in her big, overachieving family, but she'd never doubted that they'd loved her.

She knew they all missed her. Her renowned human-rights lawyer mother, her billionaire construction company CEO father, and her three siblings. Her two sisters were doctors, and her brother was a hotshot entrepreneur. And then there'd been Mia, the baby. She'd had so many careers that she'd always left her family baffled and confused.

She jumped down the last few steps, and the sound of a crash and the splintering of wood ahead made her pick up speed. Mia had never found her perfect career. Her last job had been as a spaceship pilot, and she'd liked it, and was good at it. She might have even stuck at it this time...if she hadn't been snatched by the Thraxian slavers

For a second, her stomach did a slow, jittering roll. She remembered the terrible moment the alien ship had filled her viewscreen—the screams, the horrible crunch of metal, the desperate whine of failing engines.

She shook her head, shaking the images away. At the end of the hall, two guards stood near a cell. Both were dressed in fighting leathers, muscled chests bare, and gray cloaks falling down their backs. Swords were sheathed at their sides. The younger guard had a concerned look on his face, but the older one was stone-faced, his hard gaze on the cell.

From inside came another wild roar, followed by a crash.

The young guard looked up, relief crossing his face. "Hi, Mia."

"Open the door," she asked.

The older guard frowned at her. "He's bad tonight. He's not responding at all. I don't think you should go in there."

"Open the door, please," she said calmly.

The man hesitated, before he reluctantly unlocked the door. Mia stepped into the cell.

It was a large, simple space, but comfortable. There was a doorway into the adjoining bathroom, a bunk pressed against the back wall, and a table and chairs—or the remains of them, at least. They were now mostly splintered shards.

And in the center of the room, was one wild, out-of-control, blue-skinned alien.

God, he was something to look at. He towered over her, although that wasn't unusual on this planet. Most people around here were way over her own five foot, one-and-a-half inches. He had dark-blue skin, and his muscled chest and arms were covered in what looked like black, swirling tattoos. But Mia knew he'd been born with the markings, and they were as much a part of him as his skin. And fascinatingly enough, the designs changed with his mood.

Like right now. The marks were turning dark black, the way they always did when he was in a rage.

And muscles. He had so many muscles. At the moment, they were huge and bulging. His long, black hair was in a tangle, and a dark beard covered his face.

There was no doubting he was scary and dangerous, but she couldn't pull her gaze off him.

"Vek."

He spun. His face was contorted, his chest heaving. His golden eyes glowed with a fierce light.

"It's Mia." She kept her voice low, calm. "You're safe."

He showed no hint of recognition. He growled, then spun, and slammed his fist into the stone wall. A dusty cloud of pulverized rock filled the air.

Sympathy flooded her. He'd been captured as a boy, and forced into the underground fight rings. He'd had a lifetime of being pumped full of drugs to increase his aggression, and being forced to participate in fights to the death.

There had been no hugs, no loving touches, no simple decency for Vek.

But he'd survived. Just like she had.

Despite an upbringing that would turn the gentlest soul into a murderous killer, he'd saved her. Twice.

Now Mia was returning the favor. She took a step closer. "You're in the House of Galen, and—"

He charged.

Mia knew the intimidation tactic, and held her ground. His big body pressed against her, and he loomed over her, his hot breath ruffling her short hair. He was over a foot taller than her, and he always made her feel so tiny. He lowered his head, making a low growl again in his throat. Involuntarily, she took one step back, and felt the stone wall hit her shoulder blades.

Vek pressed his face to the side of her neck and drew in a long breath.

"It's me," she murmured. "You're okay, Vek."

Another growl, but it was quieter, less furious.

He pressed his arms to the wall above her head, caging her in. She forced herself to stay calm, but she was always conscious of the fact that with one simple swipe of his huge hand, he could snap her like a twig.

Vek breathed deep, and she felt the brush of his warm lips on her skin. She shivered.

God, now was not the time for her body to remind her that she was insanely attracted to a wild, alien man with blue skin.

"Vek?"

His big body shuddered. "Mia."

His voice was deep and guttural, still rusty from the fact that he hadn't talked much in years.

"That's right." She raised her hand, and slowly stroked one huge bicep.

Suddenly, he moved, and his huge arms engulfed her. He pulled her close. "Mia."

ANGER. Molten-hot fury stormed through him. It was huge and unstoppable.

Vek'ker growled. He strained for some control,

grinding his teeth. He hated when his body didn't feel like his.

His body still craved the drugs it no longer received. The urges inside him never went away. He wanted to fight.

He wanted to kill.

He sucked in a deep breath, and inhaled a scent that flowed through him like water.

Her.

He registered the small weight in his arms. *Mia.*

He took a second to acknowledge her slight curves, and look at the shining cap of golden hair on her head. She smelled so good. Just her scent alone quieted the writhing, horrid mass of emotions inside him.

She lifted her face up to him and smiled. "Feeling better?"

Vek pressed his face against her hair.

"Mia," a deep, male voice said.

Vek tensed and spun. He pulled her closer to his chest.

"I'm fine, Galen," Mia said.

The man standing on the other side of the bars was tall and muscled. He wore leather trousers, and a sleek, black shirt that molded over every ridge and rope of muscle in his chest. A black cloak fell from his shoulders, and a black patch covered his left eye. He had a rugged, scarred face.

Vek was used to assessing opponents in an instant. His survival had depended on it. In the ring, he knew that a missing eye could be used as a weakness. Take out the other eye, and it would leave this man blind and vulnerable. A red haze covered Vek's vision. *Kill or be killed.*

But the man had a powerful body, and the hilt of a large sword was visible over his shoulder, sheathed on his back. He also had a calm, icy gaze that was calculating, cunning.

He was a fighter, and he would not be easy prey.

"I'm not sure I agree with you," the man said. "Maybe step out for a bit."

Galen. Vek remembered through the haze that the man's name was Galen.

He was trying to take Mia away.

"Mine." Vek spun and heard Mia gasp. He pulled her closer and moved to the back wall of his cell, sliding down to sit on the floor. He pulled her onto his lap, and buried his face in her hair.

"I'm okay. I'm okay," she called out. "Just give us a minute."

"A minute," Galen growled. "If you get hurt, I have a house full of Earth women who'll want my blood." In a whirl of his cloak, he was gone.

"Calm down, Vek. We're okay." Mia shifted against him.

Vek lifted his head and saw she was staring into his face. She had blue eyes the color of his skin.

She was so small. All the women of Earth were. He remembered that she'd been abducted, as well. Like him, she'd had her freedom stolen, lost any chance to return to her homeworld, and she'd been hurt. He growled.

She cupped his cheek, running her fingers through

his beard. "This is getting even longer. I will get you to agree to shave it off, one of these days."

He tilted his head, absorbing the feel of her caress. She didn't look at him like he was a monster. She looked at him like she enjoyed what she saw. He felt his cock stir, and confusion hit him. Deep in the center of him, every cell of his being was screaming for more of Mia.

Vek had never been with a woman. For years, all his sexual need had been channeled by the drugs into a fighting rage. Sometimes, he'd listen to prisoners coupling in the dark of night, and sometimes he'd stroked himself. But mostly, when need had ridden him hard, he'd just fought and spilled blood, not seed.

Until he'd been led out into the ring and he'd seen this tiny woman on the sand.

He frowned. He had no idea what to do about it.

"I have something for you." Mia pulled something from her pocket and held it up. "*Grezzo*. It's *almost* like chocolate from Earth. It's delicious."

Vek was still wary about eating. In the past, his food had often been spiked with drugs. But he trusted Mia.

She pressed the small brown square to his lips, and he opened his mouth. He chewed, and flavor exploded across his tongue. It tasted so good. Better than the rotten meat he'd been fed in the fight rings. Even better than the meals here at the House of Galen.

They sat quietly for a while.

"Bad night?" she asked quietly. "Did you have nightmares?"

His sleep was hardly ever restful. For so many years, he couldn't sleep deeply, for fear of someone attacking him. And when he did sleep, he saw the faces of all the people he'd been forced to kill. Saw their blood spraying on the sand. He shrugged a shoulder.

"The nightmares will pass in time," she said. "Mine are much better."

"I would take your nightmares, if I could."

"You have enough of your own." She leaned into him. "The House of Galen has an arena fight tomorrow—or probably today, now. I asked Galen if you could come and watch, and he approved it." She glanced at the bars. "If you'd like to come, I'll convince him not to change his mind."

A chance to watch a fair fight intrigued Vek. He knew that Kor Magna's arena was famous, and that spectators came from many different planets. It was also a chance to breathe fresh air.

"They aren't fights to the death," she reassured him. "Just House versus House, in a display of strength and prowess. You have to try and stay calm, and I'll be right beside you."

Most of all, it would be a chance to be with Mia.

Vek pushed down the aggression churning through him and nodded.

She rewarded him with a brilliant smile. "Good. We'll have fun. Now...how about I sing for you?"

His chest tightened. He loved when Mia sang.

She started singing, her voice rising and falling. The words didn't always make sense to him, but really, he just liked the sound of her pretty voice.

Vek shifted her onto the floor beside him, and then lay down to rest his head in her lap. He gripped one of her calves, liking the feel of her skin under his hand. She stroked his hair, and started another song.

One by one, his muscles relaxed, and his breathing evened out. He fell asleep to the sound of her voice. And there were no more nightmares.

CHAPTER TWO

Mia shimmied her hips to the music floating through her room. Nothing like a little classic Rolling Stones to get the blood pumping.

She was so grateful to Harper for getting her some music from Earth. Mia hated to think how much her friend had paid the local information merchant, Zhim, for the songs. She looked into the mirror in her bathroom, running her hands through her short, blonde hair. It was time to get Vek for the arena fight.

Her fingers brushed over a scar at her temple, hidden by her hair. It was where Catalyst had plugged her into his computer. The crazed madman had used people to power his system. Her mouth went dry and she swallowed, rubbing the scar. She was free and Catalyst was dead. She repeated the words like a mantra.

Mia grabbed some earrings and slipped them into her ears. God, it felt strange to have *things*. For months, she'd worn the plain, shapeless outfits the Thraxians had forced on her. It was silly to wonder if Vek would like them, or the way she'd fluffed her damn hair. The man had been locked up and forced to kill for years. She was pretty sure he didn't notice clothes or accessories.

The beat of the music caught her and she closed her eyes, belting out the words. She'd always loved music, from the moment her mother had forced her to learn piano and violin. Of course, Mia had preferred singing and rock and roll. She smiled. She'd always been scribbling down lyrics she'd never dared show anyone, dreaming of being a singer.

She swayed and sang, her chest filled with all the good emotions she'd been missing for so long.

Then she opened her eyes, and her gaze fell on the dangle of the earrings. Her singing cut off and she heard the tinkle of the pretty stones. Pain shot through her. She'd bought them from the underground markets with Dayna and Winter, after the three of them had been freed from the fight rings. Mia pressed her hands to the sink and closed her eyes.

Dayna and Winter had been passengers on Mia's ship to Fortuna Space Station—the research station that had orbited Jupiter. It had been an uneventful, routine supply run...until the ugly, spike-covered Thraxian ship had appeared. It had already attacked the space station and destroyed it.

After Mia's ship had been attacked and they'd been taken, those two women had become her lifeline. First, during their captivity on the Thraxian ship, and then when they'd been condemned to the underground fight rings.

Dayna, a former police detective, had been fierce. She'd held them together and kept them alive when hope had faded. Winter had been blinded by the Thraxians' experiments, and Mia had been beaten more times than she could count. Dayna had been the only one of them trained to fight, and she used her skills and sensible, logical head to protect them.

Now, she was missing. They'd all been snatched in broad daylight, right from the House of Galen, and while Mia and Winter had been rescued, Dayna was still out there, somewhere.

Or dead.

No. She was alive. Mia had to believe that. Wherever Dayna was, she'd be fighting to survive and working to escape. And they also knew there was another human woman out there, too—Ryan. The woman had aided the House of Galen in rescuing Mia. Mia vowed they'd find both the women.

They'd bring them both home.

The Stones had given way to U2, jerking Mia from her thoughts. She moved over to the tiny device she'd been given to play the eclectic collection of Earth songs and shut it off. She needed to get Vek. Pushing away the sadness and frustration, she headed out. She passed two House of Galen workers, who both smiled warmly at her. Mia smiled back, and hurried down to the cells.

She hated that Vek was still imprisoned, but she knew it was necessary, for his safety, as well as everyone else's. For now, at least.

But for the next few hours, she was springing him. They were going to watch the fight and enjoy some time together. She thought of her friends again, and her steps faltered. She reminded herself that Galen had people continuously searching for Dayna and Ryan, so Mia just had to wrangle some patience and wait. Which sucked.

She arrived at Vek's cell, nodding at the guards. Inside, she saw Vek was in control of his emotions, but pacing.

"Hi, Vek."

"Mia." His head lifted. His golden eyes were clear today and he looked as relaxed as Vek could get.

"Excited to see the arena?"

He nodded. The guard opened the door, and Mia waved Vek out into the hall.

"Good," she said. "It's my first fight since—" her smile slipped "—I got back."

She saw Vek's body tense. "Since you were taken from the walls of the House of Galen by the Srinar and sold to Catalyst," he growled.

Her gut churned at the thought of the man. Vek said the aliens' name like he'd sunk his teeth into something nasty. She felt the anger pumping off him.

The deformed Srinar had run the underground fight rings. She knew that Vek hated them just as much as she did.

Mia reached out. "Hey." She stroked his arm. "We're both okay. You helped rescue me, and I'm right here, free and healthy, because of you."

He gave her a jerky nod.

She stroked his skin and the corded muscles of his arms. Pure strength. That was Vek. She watched as his markings darkened under her touch. She had to admit, touching Vek calmed her, as well. He was strong, protective, and she knew he'd always come for her, no matter what.

"You should be afraid of me," he said.

She blinked. "Never."

"Even now, people are afraid or wary of me." He glanced at the nearby guards, who were watching him like hawks.

She knew it was true. His wild rages had people wary, and that was understandable. "I'm not afraid." She stepped closer, pressing her hands to his bare chest. "So, shall we go and watch the fight?"

A single nod.

Mia looped her arm through his and led him down the corridor. "We'll eat some salty *mahiz*, and listen to Rory's hilarious running commentary." Which usually involved lots of drooling over the gladiator the woman was head-over-heels in love with.

"Rory talks too much," Vek said.

Mia laughed. Rory, a fellow human survivor, was never afraid to speak her mind. "That she does."

Mia pressed her palm to his arm. Vek stared at it for a second, before he placed his large hand over hers. She looked up into golden eyes that made her think of old, polished pirate treasure. Heat radiated off his powerful body, and she realized he was extremely tense. She stroked his wrist, feeling the tick of his pulse.

God, she really wished that his face wasn't hidden by the beard. She wanted to see all of him. It didn't matter if others were afraid of him, she wasn't.

Not that her feelings toward him were all pure. She

could admit privately to herself that she had the strongest urge to climb his big, hard body, wrap her legs around him, and drive them both wild. *Down, girl.*

"You're safe with me," she murmured.

He released a shuddering breath and nodded.

"We don't have to go to the arena. We can stay here and play cards. I have another game I want to teach you."

His golden gaze was unwavering. "I would like to accompany you to the fight."

She smiled. "Good. Let's go."

AS THEY WALKED through the corridors of the House of Galen, Vek studied their surroundings. He hadn't spent a lot of time out of his cell.

It didn't take much for him to see the place was well run. While the decorations weren't ostentatious, the place was scrupulously clean, everything was in order, and there were quiet signs of wealth. He could see that from the quality of the gladiators' harnesses and weapons alone.

But he wouldn't forget that the House of Galen had been attacked, and Mia and the other women stolen from these very walls. One hand curled into a fist. He would protect her. Wherever they were, whatever they were doing, he would always defend Mia.

They turned another corner and, as always, he felt that wild rage that never went away churning in his gut. Galen's healers had said it was caused by the years of being pumped with drugs by the Srinar. The healers had no idea if it would ever stop.

He searched for a distraction. "You are well, Mia? After what Catalyst did to you?"

Her step faltered, and Vek mentally cursed himself.

She recovered quickly. "Yes. I have some missing memories from my time in Catalyst's lair. The healers keep scanning my brain, but they tell me everything looks fine. The scars I have are very faint and hidden by my hair—" she swallowed "—but I'm still a bit freaked about being plugged into his system. The thought of cables sticking into my body..." She shuddered. "I'm glad I can't remember it, but then I wonder if the images from my imagination are worse."

"I have many missing memories, as well," he said.

She squeezed his hand. "I just remind myself that I'm safe and free." Sadness crossed her face.

"You are thinking of your friends."

She nodded and turned them down another corridor. "Dayna and Ryan are still missing. They're out there, somewhere."

Her voice was so sad and it stabbed through him. He wanted to take her pain away, comfort her.

But he didn't know how to do that. He'd never comforted anyone before. He squeezed her hand, like she'd done to his.

She forced a smile. "For the next few hours, let's go and enjoy the show in the arena."

They exited out the solid double doors of the House of Galen. The guards eyed him warily, but Vek ignored them. Mia led him down one of the public corridors, and now Vek tensed. There were so many people in the small space. Lots of different smells melded together, clogging up his senses. A few people sent him curious, cautious looks.

He heard a low, distant noise, like thunder, that he recognized all too well. It made the muscles in his shoulders tense even more. It was the roar of a restless, hungry crowd. He slowed his pace.

"Vek?" Mia pulled him to a halt.

"The crowd..."

"Yes, they make a lot of noise. But remember, no one dies in this arena."

He dragged in a breath. "I know." He urged her on, following her up some steps.

The next moment, she pulled him out a door, and the wind hit his face.

Vek jerked to a stop. Sensations cascaded over him like a flood. The bright, afternoon sunlight from the planet's dual suns. The mix of smells—sweat, different species, cooking food. Overwhelming sound—the stomping feet and shouts of an impatient crowd. He blinked, confused, for a second. Usually the roar of a crowd like this meant he had to kill.

"Vek." Mia pressed a hand to his chest. "Maybe this wasn't such a good idea."

He gripped her like a lifeline and pulled in some deep breaths. He lifted his face to the sky. The golden light warmed his skin, a fresh breeze ruffled his hair, and the scent of Mia pushed out everything else. The tension within him eased by the tiniest fraction.

"I want to watch the fight," he said. "If you'll stay by my side."

Her fingers flexed on his skin. "Of course, I will."

Gripping his hand again, she led him down the next set of steps, passing the crowded tiers of seating. The huge arena was made of old stone, that Vek knew would show the wear of thousands, perhaps millions, of spectators. Every seat was filled, and the place was packed with people.

Mia led him right down close to the railing that surrounded the huge, sand-covered central arena floor. No gladiators were out on the sand yet.

He saw some of the Earth women sitting in the House of Galen seats. A redheaded woman spotted them and waved wildly.

"You'll enjoy this." Mia squeezed his fingers. "And I'm going to be with you for all of it."

CHAPTER THREE

"Hi," Mia called out to the other women.

The group turned to look at them. Redheaded Rory, blonde, curvy Regan, cool, contained Madeline, and a smiling, dark-haired Winter. All strong, courageous women, who'd survived their abduction and found a place at the House of Galen.

Only Harper and the single human man, Blaine, were missing. That was because they were down in the tunnels, preparing to fight in the arena—both of them now House of Galen gladiators.

Beside Mia, Vek was still, his broad shoulders hunched. She swallowed, wishing she could ease his uncertainty.

"Hiya, Vek." Rory patted one of the stone benches beside her. "You are in for a hell of a show tonight."

Mia tugged him over to the seats. The arena rumbled with conversation, punctuated by the occasional laugh or shout. Food vendors hawked their wares and traversed the staircases, as everyone waited for the two Houses to arrive. Mia noticed Vek staring at Rory's huge, rounded belly.

"You are with child." His tone was curious.

"Yep, I'm about to pop." Rory patted the mound. "With one very large, half human, half Antarian baby gladiator."

"Nervous?" Mia asked.

"Nope." Rory's smile was wide and pleased. "Excited. Besides, Kace is nervous enough for both of us."

Mia thought of the tall, disciplined gladiator. He was *very* protective of his human mate.

Vek's gaze moved to scan the crowd. He was still vibrating with tension, and she placed her hand on his hard thigh. She felt his muscles release a fraction.

"Remember, these fights are about pitting skill against skill," she said. "The gladiators do get injured, but the gladiator houses have very good medical teams. Galen spends a small fortune on his Hermia healers and the technology they use."

Vek gave her a small nod.

"And there are no projectile weapons in the arena," Rory added from the other side of Vek. "Everything is close combat."

"Good evening," a deep voice said from behind them.

Vek tensed again, and they both looked back. Galen swept into the seat behind them, his black cloak swinging out around him. He nodded, the imperator's watchful gaze unswervingly on Vek.

Mia realized that Galen wasn't just there to watch the fight, but to keep an eye on Vek. The way that Vek's golden eyes flashed told her that he understood the same thing.

Her jaw tightened. If they didn't start trusting Vek, he'd never be able to move past the rages and discomfort, and get on with his new life. Of course, he was still adjusting to everything, but she hated that everyone watched him like he was a danger.

Suddenly, there was the clank of metal gates rising. Vek shot to his feet, looking ready to pounce. Down on the arena floor, gates on either side were opening.

"It's just the gladiators arriving." She ran her hand down his arm. "I'm here, Vek." God, that sound had to remind him of the fight rings. She should never have brought him here. "If you want to go, just tell me." She slid her hand down to his, entwining their fingers.

Vek stared down at the sand below, then back at Mia. Then, after a tense moment, he sat back down in his seat.

On the arena floor, the House of Galen gladiators strode out onto the sand. The crowd went wild.

Raiden was in the lead, with Harper beside him. Mia smiled. They made a striking pair. Raiden with his oil-slicked body covered in a multitude of interesting tattoos, and his red cloak falling from his broad shoulders. Harper's dark hair was braided, her body clothed in tight-fitting leather, two swords clutched in her hands.

Next came big, wild Thorin, and tall, clean-cut Kace. Thorin raised his huge battle axe to the crowd, egging on their cheers. Kace was stone-faced, holding a long staff with experienced hands. Right behind the pair were Saff and Blaine. From the stands, Mia could barely tell Blaine was human. The man looked every inch the gladiator, with his dark skin, muscled body and leather harness crossing his chest. His lover, Saff, strode beside him. The woman was magnificent—tall, toned, with a mass of dark braids falling around her strong face.

The final pair were Lore and Nero. Lore was grinning, all charm and good looks, while Nero was scowling. Lore was a showman at heart, while Nero was a barbarian hunter. Both men paused to look at the stands, their gazes zeroing in on the House of Galen seats. Madeline and Winter moved to the railing, waving at their men.

The announcers shouted, trying to be heard above the roar of the crowd, announcing the opposing gladiator House.

Huge, beast-like aliens entered on the far side of the arena. Mia gaped. They were all enormous, with a light covering of silver-gray fur, and four powerful arms. Each one carried multiple weapons.

"The House of Zeringei," Galen said. "Fierce opponents."

The Zeringei all wore elaborate helmets, with plumes of different-colored fur on top. A siren wailed across the arena. *Fight time.*

The House of Galen gladiators rushed forward, weapons up. Mia's heart lodged in her throat.

"Our gladiators are smaller, faster, more agile," Vek said. "They will use that to their advantage."

Harper leaped into the air, right over the head of the lead Zeringei. As the alien looked up to watch her, Raiden came straight at him, cutting him down.

Swords clashed, and axes hit staffs. Mia watched the

blur of movements as gladiators ducked and weaved. Vek was right. The House of Galen gladiators were using their increased agility and speed to run rings around the larger, slower Zeringei.

However, the Zeringei gladiators were powerful, and carrying twice the weaponry. She saw Thorin take a hit, the big man flying backward onto the sand. Nearby, Regan leaped to her feet with a gasp.

But Thorin rose and shook his head. Blood covered his chest, his scales showing on his skin, and, with a roar, he charged back into the fight. Regan loudly released a breath and sat back down.

Vek leaned forward in his seat, gripping the railing in front of them. As the battle progressed, he slowly relaxed, his curious gaze taking in the competition.

Mia smiled. She'd been right. She'd known he'd enjoy it.

They watched Saff and Blaine work together, taking down a Zeringei holding four swords. Blaine got nicked once, but didn't even react. Soon, the Zeringei gladiator was lying on the sand, flat on his back.

"Your gladiators are well-trained," Vek said.

"I know," Galen answered.

"Who wants a snack?" Mia stood. She spotted a food vendor heading down the steps in their direction. She loved the salty, popcorn-like snack they sold at the fights. Plus, she'd made it her mission to introduce Vek to new foods. When he'd first come to the House of Galen, he'd only eaten meat, and had been too cautious to try new things.

But she'd seen the pleasure in his eyes, every time she made him try something tasty.

"Two for me," Rory answered.

Madeline shook her head. "All you do is eat."

"Hey, I'm eating for two. And one of us is hungry all the darn time."

The other women called out their orders, while Galen just shook his head.

When Vek stood as well, with a frown on his face, Mia patted his shoulder. "I'm only going to be gone for a minute. See, the vendor's right there. I'll be right back."

Vek studied the vendor, then nodded. He sat and looked back to the fight.

Mia pulled out a small token from her pocket. It was a polished coin, with the head of a helmeted gladiator in profile carved on it. The symbol of the House of Galen. On Carthago, it acted as the equivalent of an Earth credit card.

Mia waited patiently, as the vendor served the small crowd forming around him.

"You are very small," a deep voice said.

Mia turned her head and looked up. Way up. Damn, the man was tall. A huge, pale-skinned alien towered over her. He wore a pair of blue trousers and no shirt. He was heavily muscled, and she suddenly blinked, as she realized what she was seeing. His skin was translucent. She could see organs pulsing and beating inside him. *Ew.*

From the bulk of his body and the way he held himself, she knew he was a gladiator.

"Yes. And you're very big." She turned back to the vendor.

"I'm big everywhere," the man drawled, his hot breath brushing the back of Mia's neck. "You are *so* small. Can you even take a man?"

Mia stiffened. "I'm not interested, buddy." She stared at the vendor. *Come on.* There was only one other customer before her.

"I am very interested, small woman." He reached out and stroked her hair. "I could make you interested."

Memories shot into Mia like pieces of space shrapnel. The Thraxian guards on their ship, the Srinar guards in the underground fight rings. She hadn't been raped or sexually assaulted, but the fear had been a constant companion. As it was, she'd suffered some rough fondling and slimy gazes.

But she wasn't a damn prisoner anymore. She elbowed the man, hard. "Back. Off."

The vendor turned to her with a smile, but as he saw the big alien hassling her, his smile dissolved.

"I need nine bags of *mahiz*, please," Mia said.

"I want you," the persistent alien said.

She glanced back over her shoulder, anger flaring. "Well, that's not your decision, asshole."

Suddenly, he snaked a hand around her body and clamped onto one of her breasts. She hissed out a furious breath.

Before Mia could do anything else, a deep growl echoed around them.

She stiffened. *Oh, no.*

Vek charged into view, and tackled the pale-skinned alien. Star-shaped *mahiz* flew everywhere and people screamed. The crowd drew back, and Mia spotted Vek on top of the alien, pummeling him.

"Vek." Galen's deep voice. "Let him go."

Vek looked up, his golden eyes glowing.

"Vek, babe." Mia knelt beside him. "I'm okay."

"He touched you," Vek growled. "Kill." The last word was almost unintelligible.

The alien beneath him whimpered, thick, white fluid oozing from his nose.

Mia sniffed. "I think he got what he deserved. I'm hungry, and I'd like to sit with you and enjoy the fight."

Vek remained in place, vibrating with contained fury, one fist still lifted, aimed at the alien's jaw. Then with a growl, he pushed away from the man.

House of Galen guards in gray-and-red cloaks appeared.

Galen nodded. "Take him. Let's remind others what happens when you touch someone under the protection of the House of Galen."

"I didn't know she was House of Galen," the alien spluttered frantically, as he was dragged to his feet. "I didn't know she had a drakking feral bodyguard—"

Galen took one menacing step forward. "Say one more word, and I will deal with you myself."

The alien's mouth snapped shut.

"Come on," Mia tugged on Vek's arm. "Let's get back to our seats."

Vek reluctantly followed her. A moment later, the vendor reappeared, handing out their snacks.

Mia blew out a breath, letting the adrenaline from the ugly incident flow out of her. She picked up some *mahiz*. "Try this." She pressed some of the snack to Vek's lips. "You'll like it."

He took it from her, his beard and lips brushing her fingers. A small, electric zing zipped through her body. From what she could tell, he had nice lips.

He chewed on the snack and, from the way he tilted his head, she realized that he liked it. He nodded, taking some more. Then his gaze moved back to the fight.

Mia found her gaze drifting up to the evening sky above Kor Magna. The setting suns painted one horizon gold, while on the other, the moon was rising. It was larger than Earth's moon—big and bright. It made her think of Dayna and Ryan. Were they looking up at the sky right now, too? Where were they?

"The House of Galen fighters are superior," Vek said, a hint of approval in his voice.

"Hell yes, they are," Rory called out.

In the center of the arena, the fight was almost over. Most of the Zeringei gladiators were down and injured. There was only one left, battling against Raiden and Harper.

The remaining Zeringei went down. He tried to get back up, but collapsed again. Lore stepped into the middle of the arena and raised his hands. Flames flickered up his arms, and he tossed fireworks into the sky. They exploded outward, in a dizzying rush of color.

Vek flinched, but Mia pressed into his side. "Aren't they beautiful?"

On the other side of Rory, Madeline was smiling. Mia could hardly believe that the contained, composed former space station commander had fallen in love with a charming extrovert like Lore.

The siren sounded again, echoing off the stone, and blending with the shouts of the crowd. The House of Galen gladiators were the winners.

The women all jumped up, cheering and smiling.

Mia smiled and looked at Vek. He looked the most relaxed she'd seen him in a long time.

But sensing something, she glanced back. Galen wasn't celebrating. Instead, he was reading a piece of heavy paper. A young boy stood nearby, hopping energetically from foot to foot. He was clearly a message runner.

Galen's jaw had gone tight.

"What's wrong?" Mia's heart knocked hard in her chest.

The imperator lifted his head, his single eye meeting hers. It was a frigid, icy blue. "It's a message from Zhim."

Mia tensed, her chest going tight. The information merchant had to have news. "Dayna? Ryan?"

Galen nodded. "He's found something. He's asked that we go to his apartment in the District to discuss it."

Mia leaned forward. "I'm coming."

Galen remained silent.

"I need to, Galen. I...I need to help find them."

"I go with Mia," Vek said.

A muscle ticked in Galen's jaw. "No one appears to remember who the imperator is around here anymore." But he gave a curt nod. "Fine. I need some gladiators to accompany us, but you can come."

VEK STAYED close to Mia as they exited the arena.

Galen strode ahead, flanked by Nero and Lore. Both men had showered and changed after their fight.

Night had fallen, but there were so many bright lights in this part of the city that it was nearly as bright as day. Vek frowned, staring at the huge, slick buildings that touched the sky. They were all crowded together, and he didn't like it. Not one bit. There were too many people clogging the streets. And there were so many smells, all of them melding together and confusing his senses.

"This is the District," Mia said. "It's the home of decadence. Filled with every kind of establishment to fulfil every desire. The casinos are the biggest draw, after the arena, of course. People come for the fights, and get lured into spending more money here."

Vek had accompanied the gladiators into the city once before, to help track Mia when she was missing. They'd avoided the District, but he'd still disliked the trip. His lip curled. The District sounded as bad as it smelled. But then Mia's sweet scent hit him, and he dragged it in like a lifeline.

Soon, they reached a tall building, and Galen led them inside. Their boots thudded on the shiny, tiled floor, and when they reached the doors to what looked like a glass bubble attached to the building, the gladiators entered.

Vek balked. "No."

Mia held out a hand to keep the door open. "It's fine, Vek. It's called an elevator. A carriage that travels up the building. Zhim's apartment is on the very top floor and it'll take too long to walk up." Her nose wrinkled. "Of course, the man lives on the top floor."

Vek did not want to step into the small space. The idea of being trapped in the glass bubble made his eye twitch. He pulled in a breath, and glanced at the gladiators, waiting patiently inside. Then he stared into Mia's face. Keeping his gaze on hers, he forced himself to walk through the doors. He clenched his hands as the doors closed. He hated this carriage thing.

They whizzed upward and Vek swallowed a growl. Mia stepped closer and, before he knew it, the elevator slowed, and the doors slid open.

He blew out a short breath.

A tall, lean man, with long, dark hair was waiting for them. He wore a flowing, white shirt, and loose, black pants. Behind him was a large balcony, that allowed for a dramatic view over the sparkling city lights.

"Oh?" The man's gaze zeroed in on Vek. His eyes were black, with a mix of brilliant-blue and green sprinkled through them. "You brought a friend. I'm Zhim."

"This is Vek'ker," Galen said.

"Yes, the blue beast-man from the Srinar's underground fight rings. My records show you had an unparalleled number of kills."

Vek tensed. He didn't like this man knowing things about him, especially the number of people he'd been forced to kill.

Mia stepped in front of Vek. The information merchant's gaze moved to her.

"Mia Renee Ross of Earth," Zhim said. "Starship pilot, among many other short-lived careers."

"Zhim," Mia said. "Arrogant, alien-tech genius, with poor manners."

Zhim laughed. "Oh, I like you."

Vek let out a low growl, stepping forward so his chest was pressed against Mia's back. He did not like the man looking at Mia, talking to her, or liking her.

The information merchant's eyebrows raised. "That's the way it is, is it? So, what species are you, Vek'ker?"

"I do not know."

A light ignited in the man's eyes. "We'll have to rectify that."

Galen moved forward. "You have news about the women?"

Zhim's face turned serious. He waved them inside through an elegant archway. "Come."

Inside was an open, airy space, where white curtains in the windows danced in a light breeze. For a second, Vek managed to forget that he was standing on top of a giant spear of a building. He wasn't sure he liked Zhim, but he liked the man's home.

Zhim led them into a windowless room in the center of his penthouse. It looked the complete opposite of the rest of the airy apartment. This room was dark, and covered in screens and things Vek assumed were computer systems. His knowledge of that kind of thing was extremely limited.

The information merchant sat down in a large, streamlined chair behind the largest screen. "I managed to find Ryan."

Mia gasped. "You found Zaabha?"

Vek had heard the name of the vicious desert arena

whispered in the dark of the fight rings. Some fighters were known to disappear in the night, and everyone heard they were sent to Zaabha. A place with fights to the death more bloody and gory than even the fight rings.

"No, I don't know where Zaabha is," Zhim answered. "I don't know Ryan's *physical* location, but I found her signature on the system."

Strange symbols filled the screen. Vek had never been taught to read or write, but something made him suspect that he wouldn't understand this, anyway.

"I sent out tracers designed to find Ryan." Zhim grabbed a small, black glove and slipped it over his right hand. "One of them picked her up."

He touched the screen, and suddenly the stream of data appeared in the air, floating in front of the man. The green lines of text cast a glow on the man's hawkish face. He lifted the glove, and started moving his fingers through the data. It shifted and danced to his gestures.

"Wow." Mia leaned forward. "There! I can see some words in English."

"It's definitely Ryan," Zhim said.

Mia read the words aloud. "I'm alive and still in Zaabha. They are limiting my access to the system." Mia raised her head. "They must have discovered that she'd made contact with us in Catalyst's lair."

"Without her help, we would have died there," Nero added.

Galen nodded. "Most likely."

"I'm attempting to forge a visual link with her, but it's not looking like it's possible," Zhim said. "Zaabha has incredible security." He moved his fingers through the lines of text in the air, then swiped his arm across it. "I've sent out everything I could to try and make the link. I'll see if I can make contact, and we can at least have an audio-only conversation with her—"

"Hello? Is someone there?" A female voice filled the room.

Mia pushed forward. "Ryan? It's Mia."

Zhim's gaze narrowed and his fingers danced. "Ryan, my name is Zhim. I'm here with Mia, and managed to make this connection. I'm helping the House of Galen."

"Great," Ryan responded. "Mia, are you okay?"

"Thanks to you. I heard it was because of your help that the gladiators got me away from Catalyst. How are you?"

"Hanging in there." There was a weary edge to the woman's voice. "Wait a sec, let me see if I can..."

The screen on the desk blinked and an image of a woman filled it.

As Zhim reared back in shock, Vek studied the woman. She had very straight, black hair that fell to her shoulders. Her dark eyes dominated her small face, and she had pale, white skin. She looked as small as his Mia.

Zhim blinked. "You opened a visual link?"

"Sure did." Ryan smiled. "Piece of cake."

Zhim's brow creased. "Piece of cake?"

Mia grinned. "That means it was super-easy for her to do."

Ryan's smile widened. "It's so nice to see a human face again, Mia."

Mia lifted her hand to the screen. "I know how you feel."

CHAPTER FOUR

Mia stared at Ryan, emotions tumbling through her.

The woman looked to be about Mia's size, with some Japanese heritage. Her black hair hid part of her face, but it didn't quite hide the bruises mottling her cheek. Any relief Mia felt at seeing the other woman dissolved away.

"You said you were okay. Are they hurting you?"

Ryan's face went blank. "I'm fine."

Galen stepped forward. "Ryan, I'm Galen."

Ryan's gaze moved over Mia's shoulder and her eyes widened. "Wow." She glanced past the imperator, taking in Lore and Nero. "Jeez, I knew you guys were gladiators, but just...wow."

"You're being mistreated?" Galen asked.

Ryan hunched her shoulders. "Nothing I can't handle. My captors discovered that I was meddling with the comp system beyond what they'd tasked me to do. Then they realized that I'd made outside contact when I helped you guys with Catalyst. They weren't very... pleased." Ryan swallowed. "But at least they haven't thrown me in the Zaabha Arena." Horror danced in the woman's dark eyes.

"We are going to get you out," Mia said fiercely.

"Listen." Ryan leaned close to the screen. "I found Dayna."

Mia sucked in a breath. "Where?"

"I found a record of her sale. To a group called the Nerium."

Zhim frowned. "I've never heard that name. There is no one on Carthago called the Nerium."

Ryan shot him a sharp look. "Who are you, again?"

Zhim straightened. "I am Zhim, the premier information merchant on the planet. This is my system we're using to talk to you. I found you."

Ryan cocked her head. "I think I found you."

Zhim's frown deepened. "No, you didn't—"

Ryan waved a hand and ignored him. "The Nerium are based in a place called the Illusion Mountains."

Zhim crossed his arms over his chest. "There is *nothing* in the Illusion Mountains."

"Have you been there?" Ryan snapped.

"No. But I told you, I know *everything* worth knowing around here."

Ryan made a noise in the back of her throat, clearly unimpressed.

"The Illusion Mountains are a desolate place, several days' ride into the desert," Galen interjected.

"Dayna is with the Nerium in the Illusion Mountains. My captors threatened to sell me to the Nerium, as well, if I didn't stay in line. Apparently, this species stage their own sort of fight ring up there. Different from Zaabha or Kor Magna. More a game of survival."

Mia's gut clenched. This sounded bad.

"We will go to these mountains," Vek said, his hand curling on Mia's shoulder. "We'll find your friend."

Ryan turned, her gaze settling on Vek. "Wow again. An alien hunk with blue skin."

Vek stiffened a little under the scrutiny, taking a step closer to Mia.

"Zhim, I need any intel you can find on the Nerium," Galen said.

"Already on it." The information merchant tapped on another screen, scowling at Ryan's image. "I doubt we'll find anything."

"Don't pout, info-boy," Ryan said.

Zhim stiffened, but kept working.

"We need to find you, too, Ryan," Mia said. "Any luck locating exactly where Zaabha is?"

The woman shook her head. "They keep the location secret. Nothing gets out about it, and the transports to and from here are tightly controlled. I'm trying—" She broke off, looking over her shoulder.

Mia leaned forward. "What is it?"

"I thought I heard something. Info-boy, I'll send you a file of what I have on the Nerium."

"Fine," Zhim replied from between gritted teeth.

Suddenly, Ryan gasped.

Mia gripped Vek's hand. "What?"

Ryan lifted her head, her eyes stunned. "I just found

something else. A record of *another* sale of a woman to the Nerium."

Zhim stared at the screen. "I see it."

"Who?" Mia asked.

"Another woman who is listed as being from Earth," Ryan said.

Zhim nodded. "It doesn't list a name."

"It says that she was originally purchased from the Thraxians," Ryan added.

God. Mia felt like she'd been punched in the gut. Someone else had been snatched, and was lost out there on Carthago.

"Zhim, find the location of the Nerium in the Illusion Mountains," Galen said. "And then find Zaabha. I want all these women found and freed."

Mia felt the icy edge of the imperator's tone, and despite how scary he sounded, a part of her wanted to hug him.

All of a sudden, a noise came from the screen. A screech of metal, shouts, and a crash.

"Fuck," Ryan bit out. She stared straight at the screen and bit her lip. Mia saw the fear in her eyes. "My guards are coming. I need to—"

She was jerked away from the screen.

"Ryan!" Fear wrapped around Mia's throat like barbed wire.

There were shouts in a guttural, alien language that Mia's lingual implant didn't recognize. Ryan was dragged into view, and then a huge, scale-covered fist slammed into her face, sending the small woman crashing to the floor.

"*Drak.*" Zhim leaped to his feet, his gaze glued to the screen.

Suddenly, the image rocked and tilted. Then the screen went black.

"Ryan," Mia whispered brokenly.

Big arms wrapped around her, pulling her against a firm chest. Mia leaned into Vek, absorbing his strength. Then she let her tears fall.

THE WALK back to the House of Galen was somber. Vek was so focused on Mia that he barely paid any attention to the horrible sights and smells of the city.

She was upset. Her pain was like a rough scrape on his nerves, and he wanted to soothe her. He wanted to see her smile again. When she fell behind, Vek scooped her into his arms and carried her.

They entered into the arena tunnels, the gladiators' steps echoing on the stone. When they reached the large doors to the House of Galen, Mia pushed against his chest. He set her down.

She shoved a hand through her hair. "I need some air. Some space...something."

"I will come with you." Vek shot Galen a hard look. If the imperator tried to stop him, he'd have a fight on his hands. He wasn't leaving Mia alone.

Galen was frowning. "The House of Galen training arena—"

"Will still make me feel hemmed in," she finished. "I need breathing space."

"Fine." Galen's tone warned that he didn't like it. "But do not step beyond the arena walls. The central arena is empty now. I've had too many people snatched, so I'm sending two guards to watch you."

When she opened her mouth to argue, the imperator held up a hand.

"Non-negotiable. They'll stay back."

Two guards in red and gray moved closer, both men standing to attention.

Mia sighed. "Okay."

"Go. And Mia—" Galen waited until she looked up "—know that we will find your friends. I will not leave innocents to suffer."

"Thank you," Mia whispered.

Vek followed Mia up to the arena. This time, there was no thunder of voices or stamping feet. When they stepped out into the now-empty stands, he could hardly believe the difference. Most of the lights were off, and there wasn't a single noise in the place. Mia moved right to the top, sitting on the uppermost row of seats. The two House of Galen guards stayed below in the tunnel, giving them some space.

Vek could see the tops of the buildings of the District over the walls of the arena. The building where Zhim lived spiked upward, lit with blue lights. Then Vek turned to look in the opposite direction. Something tight inside him eased. That way was space and desert. Even in the darkness, he could just make out the smudge of mountains in the distance.

Mia looked up into the night sky and he followed her gaze. He stared at the large, bright moon hanging there, and for a brief second, a glimmer of a memory hit him. A single, large moon reflecting on the waters of a placid lake. Pain speared into his head in that instant, and the memory evaporated.

He looked at Mia, and saw her head was now downcast. He dropped to his knee beside her. "I vowed to you that I would find your friends, and I will."

"It's such a mess, Vek. Dayna was sold to some mystery group. Another woman we don't know is out there, somewhere. Who knows what she's suffered." Mia drew in a shuddering breath. "And Ryan... God, what if they hurt her?"

Vek reached out and tentatively touched her arm. Just like she'd touched his so many times before, to calm him.

"You don't give up," he said, trying to find words to help her. "You keep going, even when it hurts. Even when it tears you apart."

She looked up into his face. "Is that what you did? In the fight rings?"

He heard screams in his head, smelled blood, sweat, and sand. "I survived. I think your Ryan will, too."

"I sometimes wonder 'why me?'" Her voice dropped to a whisper. "Why did I get taken?"

"I wondered, too, when I first entered the fight rings." He fought to keep his muscles relaxed. "I was young, and everything was dark, frightening, and harsh." He would never, ever tell Mia the depths of the horrors he'd experienced. "But asking why is futile. There is no answer. All you can do is take each day as it comes, and move forward."

Mia leaned into him. "You're right. Thank you. I was about to dissolve into a pity party."

He looked at her blonde hair pressed to his shoulder, and the small hand resting on his forearm. Her skin was so pink and smooth, compared to his tougher blue skin and black markings.

"Vek, your markings are darkening." She frowned, her finger rubbing at one swirl. "Are you upset? Angry?"

"No." The way she stroked his skin...his cock swelled in his trousers and he swallowed a groan.

"Then why?" she asked.

"It happens whenever my emotions are...heightened."

"Heightened?" Her eyebrows rose.

"Not just anger or fear, but other emotions, too." His voice turned raspy.

"Oh?" Then pink filled her cheeks. Her gaze dropped to his lap, and her face snapped back up to meet his, her eyes wide. "*Oh.*"

Vek sucked in a deep breath. "I would never hurt you, Mia."

"I know that, Vek." She turned to him and placed a hand on his chest. He felt the warmth of her touch on his skin. "You...feel something for me?"

He pulled in her scent, and this time, it had changed to something sweeter and muskier. He stilled. "Too much."

"I feel something for you, too," she whispered. "My world is crazy, I've lost everything, but when I'm with you, I forget all that."

Every muscle in his body quivered with need.

"Have you ever kissed a woman?" she asked quietly.

He shook his head, his gaze dropping to her lips. They were pink and full. His skin was heating and he felt a tension fill the air. "Will you kiss me, Mia?"

She smiled and reached out, stroking his beard. "Yes."

She leaned up and pressed her lips to his, giving Vek the faintest taste of her. Her lips were soft and felt so good.

A burning sensation ignited inside him. A hungry, primal need.

Her mouth opened and Vek groaned. He held himself still, absorbing the sensations. Then her tongue slid inside his mouth and he barely controlled his start of surprise. The taste of her hit him. *More.* He needed more.

Mimicking her actions, he kissed her back, sliding his tongue against hers. She moaned, moving closer. With a groan, Vek pulled her onto his lap. She was so small, but felt so good pressed against him. She undulated, her hands sinking into his long hair. He kissed her harder, and she kissed him back, the kiss taking on a fierce edge.

When she pulled back, she was panting. "Well..." Her blue eyes were a little dazed. "That got out of control fast."

"You taste good, Mia. And smell good. I smell your need."

"Smell my—?" She blinked "Oh."

"I like it." He pressed his mouth to hers again.

Vek followed his instincts, and as he kissed her again, delving deep, he felt the flex of her hands on his shoulders. She made hungry little sounds in her throat that had desire pounding through him. His cock was like stone, and so incredibly painful.

Then, suddenly, he scented someone else nearby. Just as Vek stiffened, he saw the shadows behind Mia move. It wasn't Galen's guards.

Three attackers charged out of the darkness.

Vek spun, pushing Mia off his lap and thrust her behind him. The men all wore some kind of dark-green body armor, and their faces were covered with masks. They were huge, taller even than Vek, but leaner.

He let out a roar, and slammed one man away. Their scent was strong. A strange smell. Something wild, topped with the odor of freshly-turned soil.

Two men attacked him at once. Vek saw a wooden staff swing at him, and ducked. He swung out with his fists, adrenaline rushing into his veins. He'd been honed to fight, primed for it. It didn't take much for him to settle into fight mode.

He grabbed the staff and yanked it. The man stumbled with a cry, and Vek sent him flying into the empty seats. As he turned, he saw the first attacker was back on his feet, and standing with the third.

One pulled out a thick, vine-like rope. Vek growled and waited. It always made sense to know what you were dealing with, before you attacked.

But before the men made their move, Mia leaped out of the darkness and landed on the back of one of the men.

"Stay back!" Vek shouted.

He ran at the man with the rope and swung his arm. His fist slammed into the man and sent him flying into a stone wall nearby. Vek heard the crack of bone, and waited a moment to ensure the man wouldn't get back up.

When Vek spun, he saw the third attacker had managed to shake Mia free. She sailed through the air, hit the ground, and rolled.

He let out a fierce roar. No one hurt Mia.

The man rushed at him and they locked together, spinning. But Vek was enraged, and he knew he could win.

He always won.

But instead of pulling away, the man surprised Vek and pushed closer. His hand brushed Vek's neck, and he felt an all-too-familiar prick on his skin. Horror rocketed through him. No. *No!* The man had injected him with something.

Enraged, Vek flung the man off him.

"Vek!" Mia scrambled to her feet.

Vek reached up and yanked the syringe out of his skin.

She stared at it, horrified. "What did they do?"

Suddenly, heat tore through his veins, spreading through his body. It burned like acid. He felt his muscles go tense, and he threw his arms out, his fingers curling into fists.

"Vek?"

He made a strangled sound, trying to fight the feeling away. He gritted his teeth. He was losing the battle.

Hurt. Kill. Fight.

A red haze crossed his vision.

"Vek, talk to me." A small figure stepped in front of him.

He blinked, staring down into the face of a tiny woman.

Who was she? He couldn't remember. He glanced around the empty stone benches. He didn't know where he was. He didn't know who his prey was.

His mind was blank, except for the growing rage.

Behind the small woman, he saw a man rise. He wore armor.

Prey.

Hurt. Kill. Fight.

He charged past the small woman and flew at his opponent.

CHAPTER FIVE

Vek's golden eyes were glazed over with rage.

Mia lunged to the side, and watched him charge one of the attackers. He let out a sound—a wild, primal roar—that echoed across the arena and raised the hairs on the back of her neck.

He grabbed the man and lifted him off his feet. He swung the man around, dislocating the attacker's arm with one savage yank.

Mia gasped. The attacker cried out, and Vek lifted the man above his head like he weighed nothing. She knew he was strong, but whatever they'd injected him with had made him stronger, angrier, wilder.

Her heart thumping hard, she watched as Vek tossed the man upward. He sailed through the air and crashed into some seats. One of the other attackers was up and running at Vek. Vek swiveled and threw his hands out, every muscle delineated under his blue skin.

He leaped into the air, higher than she'd ever seen

him jump before, and he landed in a crouch, growling. Right in front of the attacker.

The man froze, and Mia backed away. She watched as Vek moved fast. He grabbed the attacker—whose struggles were futile—and snapped the man's neck with one vicious twist.

Mia's heart hammered against her ribs. She backed up another step.

Her movement caught Vek's attention and his head swiveled. Golden, burning-hot eyes zeroed in on her and her throat went dry. There was no recognition in them.

Just a wild, animal rage.

She took another step back, and he charged.

Mia went still, trying not to flinch. He stopped an inch from her, heat coming off him in waves. He circled around her, sniffing. She heard his breath coming fast. It matched her own. He leaned in close from behind her, his nose running down along her throat. Mia swallowed a sob.

She wanted her sweet Vek back.

She swayed, and a blue hand reached out and grabbed her arm. His grip was rough and she knew that his fingers would leave bruises.

He circled around in front of her, staring into her face. A part of her wanted to run, but she reminded herself that this was *Vek*. She wasn't abandoning him when he needed her the most. She lifted her chin.

"I know my Vek'ker is in there, somewhere."

He growled low in his throat.

All of a sudden, the thunder of footsteps echoed behind them. His body locked, and she looked over his shoulder. Galen, Raiden, and several other gladiators appeared, swords in hand.

Winter was there, as well, standing behind Nero. She was holding something in her hand. Mia recognized the casing of the sedative that they'd put together to control Vek.

No. No more drugs. He'd been hurt enough.

"Stay back," Mia said.

Vek glared at the gladiators, his chest heaving. A snarl came from his throat.

"Vek? Please come back to me." His head turned back to her, and she saw those fiery, golden eyes again.

His hand shot out and sank into her hair. He tugged her to the side, and the sting on her scalp made her eyes water.

"Let her go." Galen's voice was impossibly calm.

"Vek, that's Mia," Winter called out. "You care about her."

Vek let out a deafening roar, and his other hand came up to yank Mia closer. The rough move made her cry out.

His arms circled her and he jumped into the air. Mia swallowed a scream. They landed several tiers of seats down into the arena. She saw the others following.

"Vek."

He jumped again, leaping over several more rows. When they landed, she banged her hip and cried out.

"Stop," Raiden called out. "You're hurting her."

Mia lifted her head. She saw Raiden, Thorin, and Galen rushing at them. *Oh, no.* This wouldn't end well. "Wait!"

Vek spun to face the oncoming attack and shoved

Mia out of his way. She stumbled back, teetering on the edge of the stairs. *Dammit.*

She lost her balance, and then she was falling.

As she tumbled down the steps, bright sparks of pain burst inside her. Her hip, her side, her chest.

Something in her chest cracked, the pain stealing her breath, and behind her she could hear shouts.

Finally, she came to a stop and landed in a crumpled pile at the bottom of the stairs. From where she lay, she saw the empty sand of the arena floor through the railings. She tried to lift her head, but she couldn't move. Everything hurt. She managed to move her eyes and had a sideways view of the gladiators shooting Vek with the sedative.

She watched him throw his head back and roar. The horrible, pained sound echoed out across the arena.

Vek. Darkness and pain swallowed her.

VEK WOKE, his head throbbing and his mouth dry. He shifted and heard the clank of chains.

Fear shot through him. Was he back in the fight rings? They'd often chained him and left him for days.

"Stay calm, and I'll take the chain off."

Vek lifted his head and saw one of his wrists was chained to the wall of his cell. Galen leaned against the far wall.

"What...happened?" Vek's voice was croaky.

"You were attacked."

His head was filled with hazy memories that he

couldn't piece together. All he remembered were the out-of-control emotions. Rage. Anger. The need to fight and kill. He had fought...men in green armor.

Then he remembered the feel of soft lips on his. His first kiss.

Mia.

Vek surged up, the chain clanking. "Mia was with me."

Galen walked over and calmly unshackled him.

Vek growled at the imperator. "Where is she?"

"In Medical."

An icy chill swept through Vek. "I'll kill them all over again. What did they do to her?"

A strange, almost reluctant look crossed Galen's face. "They injected you with something. It made you lose control."

Vek froze, his chest locking. He remembered a fuzzy image of Mia tumbling down the arena stairs.

And he'd been the one who'd shoved her.

"Is she..."

"She's fine, Vek. A few bumps and bruises, and some broken ribs."

Broken ribs. He'd broken her bones. *Him.*

He was a monster.

Vek threw his head back and let out a howl of anguish.

MIA SLOWLY SHOOK off sleep and opened her eyes. She was floating in goo.

She wrinkled her nose, swirling her fingers in the blue ooze. It was the goop they had in the regen tanks in Medical. She rubbed the sticky stuff between her fingers.

"Hey, there." Winter appeared beside her. One of her eyes was a brilliant blue, while the other one was covered in a film of white. Her eyes had been damaged by the Thraxians and their experiments, but she now had full vision back in one eye. The doctor leaned over, checking a readout on the side of the tank. "All healed. You can get out now."

Mia gripped Winter's hand, and let the other woman help her out. Her muscles shook as she climbed over the edge. Winter held out a robe and Mia pulled it around her naked body.

"What happened?" she asked. "I can't remember anything."

"You were attacked." Winter's face turned serious.

Mia touched her temple, trying to remember.

The doors to Medical whooshed open, and her friends appeared. She was engulfed in hugs from Madeline, Rory, and Harper. Only Regan was missing.

"I'm fine," she told them.

"You had two broken ribs," Winter said. "But they're all healed now."

"Who attacked me?"

The women traded looks. Mia's heart thumped in her chest. What did that mean?

"Unknown assailants attacked you while you were sitting in the empty arena," Harper said. "They killed the guards Galen had sent with you."

Arena. Moonlight. Kiss. Vek.

"Vek! They injected him with something. Where is he?" Her tone turned frantic, and she scanned the room, trying to find something to wear.

"He's back in his cell," Harper said steadily.

"They attacked us," Mia said. Where were her clothes? "They went straight for him, and injected him with something. It's his worst nightmare being out of control like that."

"Mia." Harper pressed her hands to Mia's shoulders. "Vek shoved you aside, and you fell—"

"It's not *his* fault. Clothes. I need clothes." She sent Winter an imploring look.

The doctor nodded and crossed the room to a line of cabinets. She returned with some soft, loose-fitting clothes. Mia dumped the robe, uncaring that the women would see her naked. She yanked the clothes on. She had to get to Vek.

"Was it the Srinar?" Mia asked. "Did they use the same drugs on him as in the fight rings?"

Harper shook her head. "They weren't Srinar. We don't know who they were. After Galen, Raiden, and the others contained Vek and got you to Medical, the bodies of the attackers had disappeared."

"Regan took samples of the toxin from Vek," Madeline said.

Mia stilled. "Toxin?"

Rory nodded. "It wasn't a drug. It's some plant-based toxin. Regan's locked in her lab now, trying to work out what it is."

"I need to see Vek." Mia tucked her shirt into the trousers.

"I'll come with you," Harper said.

Mia shook her head. "Vek would never hurt me, Harper." She scanned them all. "Even under the influence of that drug, he didn't hurt me, except by accident. We freed him, yet we keep him in a cell, keep sedatives to drug him, and watch him like a wild beast that might turn on us. I will *not* treat him like that."

She stepped forward and the women parted. Mia hurried out of Medical. She raced down the hall, feeling a little lightheaded, but she pushed through it.

She raced down the steps and reached the cells.

But as she neared Vek's cell, the two guards stepped in front of her and blocked her way.

"I need to see him," she told them.

"It's not a good time," the female guard said.

Mia raised her voice. "I don't care if he's angry. I need to see him."

The male guard rubbed the back of his neck. "I can't let you."

Mia was done playing around and shoved against them. They didn't budge. "Why?"

"He doesn't want to see you," the woman said.

The words were like an arrow to Mia's heart. She took a step back. "What?" She looked toward the cell. From where she stood, she couldn't quite see inside. "Vek? It's Mia."

Silence.

The male guard leaned back, looking through the bars. Whatever he saw made him shake his head at her.

Mia pressed her lips together.

"It wasn't your fault, Vek. I'm okay." She sucked in a breath. "Can I come in?"

The guard looked once more, his mouth tightening. Mia saw pity in his eyes when he shook his head at her again.

Mia wrapped her arms around herself. Vek had never refused to see her. Ever. Not sure what to do next, she turned and made herself walk away.

CHAPTER SIX

Vek sat in his cell, staring at the floor. He'd been doing it for hours. He'd spent a sleepless night staring at the ceiling, so today he was planning to stare at the floor. He already knew every crack, mark, and joint.

As he'd lain on his bunk during the night, all he'd seen in his head were images of Mia's body falling. Over and over.

Every time he'd drifted off, it had morphed into images of her twisted, lifeless body on the arena sand, her blood pumping out of her.

His teeth clicked together and his jaw clenched tight. He deserved to wallow in his guilt. He'd hurt the one person who he wanted to protect.

He heard voices outside his cell. A female's voice. He cocked his head. It was Rory. He heard the rumble of the guards' voices, and seconds later, footsteps.

There was silence, and then movement at the bars. The cell door clicked open.

He smelled her before he saw her, his body flaring to life. Mia.

Vek's heart thumped in his chest. She looked as she always did—pretty face, slim body. She was wearing a simple slip of a dress in a shade of blue that matched her eyes, and left a lot of her slim legs bare. But she had her hands balled on her hips and a determined look etched on her face.

"You shouldn't be here," he growled.

"Come on," she said. "You're coming with me."

He shook his head. "It's safer if I'm locked up. Safer for everybody. Safer for you."

She stomped over to him and Vek rose to his feet.

She poked him in the chest. "They drugged you. With some unknown poison. Regan's trying to work out what, but you're not superhuman, Vek." She frowned. "Or superalien. Or whatever. If I'd been pumped full of that toxin, I would have reacted the same way. Would you have held it against me if I'd hurt you?"

He just stared at her. "Why aren't you looking at me like I'm a monster?"

"Because you're not." She reached up, her hand stroking his beard-covered jaw. "From the first moment you saw me, all you've done is stand in front of me and been my shield. You're a protector, Vek, not a monster." She stroked his beard. "It's time to stop hiding and pretending that you are one."

Warmth flooded Vek's chest. He recognized the sensation as hope. Something he hadn't felt in such a long time. Something he'd thought had been stomped out of him in the fight rings. But this small woman gave it back to him.

"My mother works as a human-rights attorney. She helps people who've had their rights abused, or denied to them. The basic things all of us deserve. She told me that some of them punish themselves, believing they don't deserve the simplest kindness. Sometimes, they do things to sabotage themselves."

He watched her steadily, emotions churning inside him.

"Don't sabotage yourself, Vek." She held her hand out to him, palm up. "Come with me."

He didn't hesitate. He put his hand in hers, and she tugged him out of the cell.

He studied the empty corridor. "Where are the guards?"

"Rory helped me. She may have insinuated the baby was coming."

Vek shook his head. These women of Earth could be devious when it suited them.

He followed Mia, as she led him up the steps and through the twists and turns of the House of Galen. They didn't exit the House, but she led him into an area he'd never been to before, up more and more stairs that curved around and around.

Then they stepped out onto a rooftop.

It was sunny, and for a second he absorbed and savored the feel of the warmth on his skin. The wind caught his hair and he smelled the desert—hot and sandy. He looked around and saw this small space was a rooftop garden. There were lush plants everywhere. Some in rows, others in pots, and several larger trees and vines, all overgrown. His senses expanded and he instantly wanted to plunge into the dappled shadows.

Mia closed the door behind them.

"What is this place?" he asked.

"Madeline organized the kitchen staff to start this garden. They grow lots of fruit, vegetables, and herbs here. Madeline said something about saving money on fresh food. Isn't it great? No one comes up here much. I thought you'd like it."

Because she knew he'd spent most of his life locked deep underground, with no sunshine, no fresh air, no plants.

She led him through some vines, and he spotted a small, clear area set up with some large cushions and a small table.

On the table, he saw an electronic device, a bowl of water, a round mirror, and several metal implements, including a sharp blade.

"Sit." She nudged him down on the pillows. Then she touched the device and music filled the air. It was the throaty sound of a woman singing. "This is an Earth singer called Adele." Mia moved back to him, her hips shimmying a little to the beat.

Vek leaned back and listened, but his gaze was on Mia's hips.

"Do you like it?"

He blinked. "What?"

"The music." She started singing, adding her voice to the song.

He could see how much she loved the music. Her

face lit up when she sang, her eyes glowed. "I like it when you sing."

She smiled at him, then reached out and touched the long strands of his black hair. "This really needs a trim."

She'd mentioned before that she wanted to cut his hair.

"I want to see the man underneath this, Vek. Let others see him, too. Let yourself see him."

Was he really hiding behind his hair? Maybe. "I would do anything for you, Mia."

She knelt on the cushion beside him. "I want you to do it for yourself." A small smile. "Although I did have some whisker burn on my jaw this morning."

Their kiss. In all the upheaval after the attack, he hadn't let himself think of that perfect moment of pleasure.

"I marked your skin?" He reached out and stroked her smooth jaw, finding a small, faint patch of redness on it. Unacceptable. "Cut my hair, Mia."

She rubbed her hands together. "You won't regret it." She twisted some fabric around his shoulders and then started wetting his hair. "I was a barber for a few months, once," she said. "So, don't worry. It was one of my many careers."

She set to work cutting his hair. *Snip. Snip. Snip.*

"Why did you have so many careers? Couldn't you find one you liked?" he asked.

"Partly. My family...they are all very smart and very driven. All overachievers. I always felt...inadequate."

He moved his head slightly to try and look at her. "Mia, you're very smart."

She straightened his head again. "Thanks, babe."

He frowned at her. "I'm full-grown, not a babe."

She smiled. "It's an endearment, Vek."

He frowned. No one had ever called him by an endearment before. A swirl of warmth flickered through his chest. She kept cutting and snipping.

"My family loves me," she continued, "and I love them all like crazy, but I guess I felt left out. I always sensed this quiet frustration from them, because I wasn't achieving my potential."

"You changed your work so much so you would never succeed and never fail."

She paused. "Damn, I think you're right. That's pretty perceptive."

"I think you are smart, Mia, but you have many other admirable qualities. Kindness, compassion, determination. And the way you sing...the emotion in it. It is extraordinary."

A beautiful smile broke over her face. "You make me sound kinda special."

"I did not see those qualities much before I met you. Nor did I ever hear music like yours."

Her hands stroked through his shortened hair. "Thanks." Her voice came out husky, then she cleared her throat. "Okay, time for the beard now."

She stepped right in front of him, trimmed his beard a little, then grabbed a pot filled with a white substance. As she rubbed it between her hands, it started to foam.

"Regan assures me this is what passes for shaving cream on Carthago." She rubbed it over his face, then started scraping at his beard with the blade.

But his attention was soon diverted, since her breasts were right at his eye level. He swallowed. They were small, but perfectly formed. Just like Mia.

Desire rose in him and he tried to clamp down on it. But she was so close, her sweet scent working into his senses, and something wild in him twisted. It wanted more.

It wasn't like the rage, it was something else.

Finally, she put the blade down, and gently wiped his jaw with a small towel. "Finished." Her voice was husky as she stepped back. She stared at his face for a long moment, and then she reached out and ran a hand over his freshly-shaven skin. He liked her touch and turned his face into her hand.

"Wow. I cannot believe what you were hiding under there." She held the mirror up.

Vek stared at the unfamiliar face.

"You're handsome, Vek. So damn handsome. Strong jaw, gorgeous lips, a little cleft in your chin." She shot him a faint smile. "I'm going to have to fight to keep the women off you."

As she moved to set the mirror down, he grabbed her wrist. "There is only one woman who stirs me."

She looked up, their gazes locking. Then her eyes drifted down to his mouth. "Vek." A husky murmur.

He pulled her closer. He wasn't exactly sure what he was doing, but he decided to follow his instincts. And right now, they were screaming at him to touch her, claim her. That Mia was his.

He tugged her onto his lap and kissed her.

She moaned, cupping his now-bare cheeks. She

rubbed her body against him and the warm center of her pressed against one of his thighs.

Her dress had ridden up. Giving into the urge, he ran a hand up one of her slim legs. "Mia."

"Do you like touching me?"

He nodded. Her hand covered his, her nails raking up his arm. He shivered.

"Do you like when I touch you?"

He nodded again. "Yes."

"You're so hard, and your skin is so hot." She drew circles on his bicep. "Enjoy the pleasure, Vek." She sounded breathless. "Whatever you want, take it."

Following the urge driving him, he spun and pressed her down on the pillows. He covered her, a primitive part of him loving having his big body caging hers. He moved down to press a kiss to one slim ankle. Then he started peppering kisses up her leg. So soft, so beautiful. He took his time, relishing every part of her. He stopped to toy with the smooth skin behind her knee, and she made a husky cry.

He looked up at her and she pushed up on her elbows, her face flushed. Then she reached for the slim straps on her shoulders and slipped them off. Her top slid down, pooling at her waist. Vek's cock surged against his trousers, and his hungry gaze went to her bare breasts. Her nipples were pink.

"Touch them," she murmured.

He reached out, his big hands closing over the small mounds. So soft and small in his huge hands. Her nipples pebbled, and he rubbed them with his thumbs. His cock was so hard and throbbing against his trousers.

"You can put your mouth on them," she said. "Kiss them, suck on my nipples."

Really? Excitement surged inside him, and he lowered his head, looking at one pink nipple. He lapped at it before sucking it into his mouth. She cried out, pushing up against his mouth. He gently squeezed her small breasts together, licking and sucking. He moved to the other one, loving the sounds she made, and the way she writhed against the cushions.

Her hands moved into his newly cut hair. There was still enough for her to hold onto tightly.

The smell of her arousal teased him. She was in need, and he wanted to satisfy her and bring her pleasure. It was his job to give Mia what she needed.

He reached down, pushing the skirt of her dress up.

"Yes," she murmured.

He uncovered her slim thighs, and then stared at the small scrap of fabric between her legs. His cock was so hard it hurt. He brushed his fingers against her underclothes and she shifted restlessly.

Vek slid a finger beneath the fabric and then jerked, tearing it off her.

She cried out, watching him with a hungry gaze. She let her legs fall apart.

Vek made an inarticulate sound. He lifted one hand and stroked the pale curls between her legs. "Pretty."

"More." Her hips lifted toward him.

He took his time exploring the soft, pink folds. He found one spot, where she was wet. The scent was tormenting him.

"Right there." Her teeth sank into her bottom lip. "Slide your finger inside me, Vek."

Drak. Vek felt his legs go weak at the thought. Gently, he sank a finger inside her.

"Yes, Vek."

She was so warm, so tight.

"Harder."

He slid his finger out and back in, giving her what she wanted. He couldn't take his gaze off her. She was the most beautiful thing he'd ever seen. He stroked her with his other hand, his fingers brushing over a small nub nestled at the top of her folds.

"Oh!" She arched up. "Right there."

"Here?" He rubbed it again.

"Yes!" She was panting. "That's my clit. It gives me pleasure."

He rubbed it again, in slippery little circles. She was writhing against his hand now.

"Mia, can I...?" He wasn't exactly sure what he was asking.

"Taste me, Vek." Her eyes glittered. "Put your mouth on me."

Yes. That was exactly what he wanted. He lowered his head and growled. Then he licked her, from the top, all the way to the bottom, and back again. The wild, mewling sounds she made drove him on. He slid his hands under her curvy buttocks and lifted her up to his mouth.

Mia threw her head back, her body twitching as he lapped at her. He was so hungry.

"My...clit." Her voice was breathless. "Suck it."

He obeyed, sucking the small nub into his mouth.

Her entire body stiffened and she screamed his name. Vek watched the pleasure suffuse her face, her mouth falling open as she rode out her release.

He smiled. This was even better than winning a fight.

She flopped back on the pillows, her skin flushed. Vek held her, stroking a hand over the smooth skin of her belly. "Mia."

"YOU SOUND HAPPY WITH YOURSELF." Mia smiled, enjoying the languid feeling filling her. "That was so good, Vek. Thank you."

He stroked his hand lower, moving gently between her thighs. He fingered her again, his gaze laser focused. "You're swollen."

"From my arousal and my orgasm."

He slid his finger inside her again, and she bit her lip.

"That's..." she cleared her throat. "That's where you'd slide your cock inside me, if we make love."

His head jerked up. "My...it would not fit here."

She smiled. "I promise you it will. When we're both ready."

Vek frowned. "I saw guards...brutalize women and some men."

She sat up, slipping the straps up on her dress. "What they did wasn't sex, Vek. That was about power and pain. This, what's between us, this is something else." She reached out and touched his mouth. "God, you have the sexiest lips. They were hidden before, but now I can see them perfectly." She rubbed her thumb over his bottom lip.

He licked the pad of her thumb. "I can still taste you."

She blushed, and reached down to push her dress down. He leaned down and pressed a kiss to her shoulder.

"Thank you, for letting me touch you."

"I should be thanking you."

"Now that I've tasted you, I'll crave more. Crave you."

Mia shivered. "I'm okay with that." Her gaze dropped to the bulge straining the front of his trousers. "And now I'm going to touch you."

His body shuddered. "I wanted to pleasure you. I don't expect—"

She pressed her finger to his lips. "Shh. I want to. Do you know how many times I've imagined touching you like this?"

Air was sawing in and out of his lungs as she opened the fastening on his trousers. She lowered the cloth down and his large cock sprang free from a patch of black hair.

Oh, he was so big and thick. She licked her lips. It was as powerful as the rest of him.

Mia took his cock in her hand and Vek groaned. It pulsed in her palm, and she curled her fingers around it, sliding up and down.

Another desperate groan ripped from him and desire fired inside Mia again. Pre-come leaked from the head of his cock, sticky on her fingers. Oh boy, she wanted to take him in her mouth and taste him.

"I want to taste you, Vek." She slid between his thighs, leaning over him. She pressed a kiss to one rock-hard thigh, and his body quivered.

"You do?"

"Yes." She licked the bulbous head of his cock, and his hips jerked up. His body was strung tight beneath her.

"Why?" The word shuddered out of him.

"Because I want you. And you want me. And it's time we both get something we want."

She lowered her head, the musky smell of him making her mouth water. She gave him a long, slow lick before pulling him in between her lips.

Mia licked and sucked as much of him into her mouth as she could. He made a strangled sound in his throat. She worked him with her mouth and tongue, loving the salty taste of him. Soon, he was groaning, loudly and desperately, his hips bucking up. He kept his hands planted in the cushions.

She reached for one large hand, and brought it to her head. His fingers tangled in the strands of her hair.

"Mia...I'm not going to last much longer."

The deep growl of his voice shivered through her. She sucked harder, taking him deeper.

A last, large groan ripped out of him. "I'm going to..." He tried to pull back.

Mia held fast, and then she felt his body shaking. He growled her name as he came, pumping his release down her throat. She swallowed it, and when he collapsed back on the cushions, she shifted, lapping at his softening cock.

When she looked up his gorgeous body, his marks were the darkest black she'd ever seen. His dazed, satisfied gaze was on her. Looking at her like she was the most amazing, most desirable woman in the galaxy.

She moved upward, pressing kisses to his skin. She touched his full lips, dragging her thumb across them, then stroked his smooth jaw. "You are incredible."

"Mia—"

A banging on the garden door broke the moment, and made Mia start.

Dammit. She wasn't ready for their time to be over. Vek tensed and leaped to his feet. Mia rose and pressed a hand to his arm. "We're in the House of Galen, remember. It's okay." She straightened her dress and motioned for him to get dressed.

She hurried over to the door, smoothing her hair. When she opened the door, Galen and Raiden stood on the other side. God, she hoped it wasn't obvious what she and Vek had been doing.

"Found you," Galen said.

"I'm sorry, Galen. I needed to get Vek out of his cell. I had to make him see that what happened wasn't his fault. He doesn't need to be caged—"

"I'm not concerned with that, Mia."

"You aren't?"

Galen lifted his gaze, and when he spotted Vek, his single eye widened slightly. "You look—"

"Like a man," Mia said.

Vek self-consciously stroked his jaw. "Mia asked to cut my hair and shave my beard."

"Suits you," Raiden said. The gladiator raised a brow. "I'd guess a few things suit you."

Mia felt heat in her cheeks. *Right.* Clearly, it was completely obvious.

"Vek," Galen said abruptly, obviously moving on. "I want to take you back to the arena to see if you can track the attackers. Nero did what he could, but he lost them in the busy hub in the lower levels. There were too many scents." Galen's face darkened. "I lost two good men and I want the sand-suckers responsible found."

"And Vek's senses are unparalleled." Mia looked up at him.

"I'll help." Vek straightened. "Whoever attacked me, hurt Mia. I want them to pay."

"Good," Galen said. "Let's go hunting."

CHAPTER SEVEN

Vek followed Galen, as the imperator led them out of the House of Galen. He tried to focus on finding the drakking aliens who'd drugged him, but he was so conscious of Mia by his side.

She'd laid down before him, naked, and let him touch her, taste her. Like a private offering just for him. Then she'd touched him and pleasured him. Even now, desire was a hungry echo that reverberated through his body. She'd given herself to him—a man who had been no more than a beast for so long.

He wanted more. Much, much more.

Galen led them up to the top level of the arena. When Vek stepped out at the spot where he and Mia had been sitting the night before, his muscles locked.

His gaze fell to the stairs, and the image of Mia falling played over again in his head. His jaw went tight.

Mia grabbed his hand and squeezed. "Not your fault."

A sound rumbled through his chest. It would be a long time before he believed that.

She leaned closer, her voice low. "Do you know what I think of when I look around here? Our first kiss."

His cock stirred, and his anger dimmed.

"Now, let's find these assholes, Vek."

He drew in a deep breath and nodded. He circled around, teased by that strange scent that he'd picked up the night before. Something like plants and dirt. Another hint of a memory flickered through his brain, but it slipped away before he could grasp it.

There was something about this scent that made his skin prickle and his gut go tight.

Following a delicate thread of the smell, he broke into a jog. He headed back into a tunnel, with Mia, Galen, and Raiden quickly following behind him.

Vek jogged through the tunnels beneath the arena. Several people were trudging through the tunnels—off-duty gladiators and workers. They were quick to get out of his way.

The scent dimmed and Vek paused. He stroked his jaw, surprised for a second to feel smooth skin. Mia shifted closer, and her scent hit him. His mind returned to the garden above. To having his mouth between Mia's legs, lapping at her beautiful taste, watching her find her release.

Giving Mia pleasure was his new favorite thing.

"Anything?" Galen asked.

The imperator's voice almost made him jerk. Vek pulled in another deep breath, filtering out Mia's scent. Taking another breath, he forced himself to focus. He circled around the space and picked up the attackers' trail again.

"The scent grew faint. But it goes this way."

They moved deeper into the tunnels, and came out in a large, open area. Several tunnels converged here, forming a hub, where arena workers and shopkeepers had small tables set up selling goods. Nearby, he smelled cooking food, and the tart scent of different ales. There were several open doorways in the walls, and he guessed they led to places where people could eat and drink.

There were so many people, and a tangled jumble of scents.

"This is where Nero lost the trail," Galen said.

Vek did several loops of the space, conscious of people staring at him. That included a number of women. Their fascinated gazes slid over his face, and then lower.

He ignored them. He'd had a lifetime of people staring at him—with fear, awe, curiosity. Some females had come to the fight cells, paying money for rough sex with fighters. Vek had never accepted the offers. He glanced over and saw Mia scowling at the females. Warmth hit his gut. His Mia was possessive.

Plants and freshly-turned soil. The smallest hint of the scent reached him, and he lifted his head. He took two steps in one direction, but the scent faded. He spun and moved in another direction. *There.* It grew stronger. He strode forward.

Mia fell in beside him. "I love watching you work."

He looked down at her. A small smile tilted her lips.

"It's amazing. You can do things that no one else can do."

He wanted to argue that it was just his enhanced senses, but a flush of pride filled his chest. He led them into what looked like an abandoned tunnel. Unlike the other brightly-lit, mostly-clean corridors, this one was dark and dank. They followed it for several paces, until the tunnel began to glow with light.

The tunnel ended at a metal grate, and through it, he saw daylight, and the city beyond. The center of the grate looked like it had been melted by something. Careful not to touch it, he arched his head and looked out. It was a good drop to the ground, but nothing life-threatening.

"They escaped through here," Vek said.

Galen stared at the melted grate, scowling. "And out into the city. They could have gone anywhere from there."

"I can try and follow the trail."

The imperator thrust his hands onto his lean hips. "It's likely they would have had a transport waiting."

Which made the trail near-impossible to follow.

"What's this?" Mia crouched and picked something up.

Vek stared at the small thing on her palm. It was a flower. Its long petals were crushed, like it had fallen, and gone under someone's boot.

Raiden moved forward and frowned at it. "It's a unique color."

Vek agreed. It was not quite red, not quite pink, not quite purple. As Mia moved her hand, the petals glittered with an iridescent sheen.

"I'm no expert on flowers," Galen said. "But I've never seen one like this before."

Vek leaned over and took a sniff of it. "And I've never scented one like this before. But it is the same scent that the attackers had."

Galen gave a single nod. "Good work, Vek. Let's get this to Regan and see if she can identify it."

"Do you think it's a clue?" Mia asked hopefully. "Do you think it'll help us find Dayna and the others?"

"It could," Galen said. "But it is best not to get your hopes up."

Vek stepped closer to Mia, touching her back. Whether or not this flower was a clue, he'd vowed to help her find her friends.

Her hand crept into his, and he folded his fingers over hers. He would keep searching for the missing women.

Whatever Mia wanted, he would get it for her.

MIA SAT IMPATIENTLY at the dining table, in the spacious living area that belonged to the high-level gladiators. She tapped her fingers restlessly on the glossy surface. Vek was sitting next to her, but he wasn't sitting very still. She felt heat pumping off his big body, and his annoyance at waiting.

She snuck a sideways look at him. He was such a fascinating blend of strength and power, with a touch of sweetness beneath. She was pretty sure no one else would agree with her when she called him sweet, but Mia saw it. He was also extremely talented with his hands and mouth. She shivered. Being the complete focus of his attention was...amazing.

Mia knew he'd give his everything as a lover, as well. She shivered again.

Hot memories from the rooftop garden peppered her head, and she pressed her thighs together. God, she couldn't believe she was crazy about a blue-skinned alien. She hadn't seen that one coming.

Vek glanced her way, his eyes glowing. "I smell your—"

She slapped a hand against his mouth. "Shush."

The door opened and Regan marched in, clutching a number of things in her arms. Galen and another man followed behind.

Mia stared at the newcomer. He looked like a desert pirate. He wore a sand-colored shirt crossed with a leather bandolier, and dark brown trousers that slicked over lean hips and long, muscular legs. Tawny hair was tied at the back of his neck and his rugged face was dominated by gold-colored eyes. They were a deep amber color, different than Vek's.

"I believe everyone knows Corsair," Galen said. "Except you haven't officially met Mia."

The man inclined his head, then looked at Mia. "I'm glad to see you've recovered from your ordeal." He gave her a gallant little bow.

Caravan Master Corsair. She knew he'd been a member of her rescue team, leading the gladiators into the desert. "Thank you."

Beside her, Vek let out a low growl. She glanced at

him and saw he was staring at Corsair with narrowed eyes. She reached out and patted his hand.

Galen turned to Regan. "Regan has an update for us."

The scientist set her things down on the table and looked around at the assembled group. "The plant Mia found in the tunnel is not native to Carthago. It is definitely the source of the toxin used to poison Vek. I've asked around the underground market, and several plant dealers that I know. Almost all of them said they'd never seen it before. But then I got lucky." A smile lit up her pretty face and she pushed a strand of her blonde hair back. "I found someone who had seen it. It's called a Neralla flower."

Galen pressed his hands to the table. "They'd seen it in the Illusion Mountains."

A hush spread over the room.

Raiden frowned. "How could it be growing in the Illusion Mountains if it isn't native?"

"My guess is that someone is planting and growing it up there," Regan said.

"The Nerium," Mia breathed. "Did Zhim find out anything more about them?"

Galen shook his head.

"Why would they attack Vek?" she asked.

"We don't know," Galen answered.

"Where are these mountains?" Mia demanded.

"That's where I come in," Corsair drawled. "I've been there before. I led my caravan across the Illusion Mountains, once. It's a dangerous, poorly-charted trek that I'd never planned to do again. The path through the mountains can be treacherous—landslides, sinkholes, or suddenly no path at all. And the weather is mercurial. It can be dry one second, and then you can have a freak storm and flash floods the next. And things up there are...strange."

"Strange?" Thorin said.

"You superstitious, Corsair?" Raiden asked with a raised brow.

Corsair lifted a shoulder. "I'm a man of the desert, Raiden. I've seen things that defy logic and definition. How do you think the mountains got their name? People and animals disappear up there. Landmarks and vegetation can change, in just hours. It's easy to get turned around and lost. And it's easy to have your entire caravan picked off, one by one, if you aren't careful. I lost several people up there."

Something flashed across his face, so briefly that Mia almost missed it. But it didn't soften her resolve. "We need to go there. We need to find Dayna."

"There's more," Galen said. "Zhim found something on Ryan."

Mia didn't like the set look on Galen's face. Her chest went tight.

"He made contact with her again?" Harper asked. "Is she okay?"

Galen released a breath. "He found a record of her sale."

"No," Mia breathed. Her captors had sold her.

"To the Nerium."

Mia could barely breathe. "So Dayna and Ryan are

both in the mountains?" She shot to her feet. "We have to—"

"We're going, Mia," Galen said. "We're planning it now."

"I'm—"

Galen held up a hand. "I'm giving the orders today."

At the imperator's deep voice, Vek stood, standing close to Mia. She saw his hot gaze was on Galen. She pressed her hand to his arm, to calm and reassure. That was all she needed, for Vek to challenge Galen.

"We'll need Vek's skills to track the Nerium into the mountains," the imperator said. "And Vek needs you, Mia."

Relief shuddered through her. He was letting her go. "When do we leave?"

"Listen," Corsair said. "I will guide you into the mountains, but you need to know it is *not* an easy trip. The mountains are tough enough, but getting to the mountains is just as hard. We will have to cross the Gargas Badlands."

"Sounds like fun," Raiden said dryly.

Corsair snorted. "It's a pockmarked, hellish area of the desert. The ground is unstable, and I've heard if you fall into a crevasse, you'll end up in a pool of lava. And that's not the worst part."

"Give it to us," Thorin growled.

"Creatures live in the Badlands. Buried under the sand. They are known as the *norkhoi,* or death borers."

Galen pinched the bridge of his nose. "Excellent."

"They burrow through the sand, pop up through the

surface, and then drag people down. They eat their victims alive."

Mia's fingers dug into Vek's skin. *Oh, God.* Dayna, Ryan, and this mysterious other woman were all lost out in that horrible place.

"We can travel by *tarnid* to the Badlands," Corsair said.

"Why not take a shuttle?" Mia asked.

Corsair shook his head. "Shuttles do not mix well with the deserts of Carthago. There are minerals in the sand that are attracted to metal and heated engines."

"It clogs them up and eats away at the metal very quickly," Galen said. "More than a few people have found their deaths crashing into the desert dunes."

"That's why the caravans are such a lucrative business," Corsair said. "Once we reach the Badlands, I'll have to guide you through on foot. And then we need to travel into the mountains on foot, as well."

"Mia," Vek said. "Perhaps it is safer if you stay—"

"No." She lifted her chin. "I'm finding my friends."

Galen gave a single, sharp nod. "Everybody prepare. We leave in the morning."

CHAPTER EIGHT

Vek ran quickly across the hot sand, enjoying the stretch of his muscles. Carthago's dual suns were scorching hot, and he felt sweat trickling down his back, but he didn't care.

He had wide-open space ahead of him. He was free, and Mia was with him.

He turned his head and watched her riding the giant, six-legged beast beside him. She had a happy look on her face. He knew she was pleased for the opportunity to help find her friends.

Around them, the rest of the House of Galen group had fanned out on their *tarnids*. Vek wrinkled his nose. He disliked the large creatures and they disliked him right back.

But he was more than happy running, and could keep up this pace for days.

They'd spent the rest of the day before preparing for the trip. He'd watched Galen and Madeline organize supplies for the desert trek. Vek had wanted to spend more time with Mia, but it had been a whirl of preparation, and she'd been busy with Harper finding clothes for the trip. Right now, Mia wore sand-colored, loose-fitting clothes, and a length of beige cloth wrapped over her head to protect her from the sun. Vek had traded his fighting leathers for loose-fitting trousers and shirt, and desert boots. His fighting forks were tucked into specially designed sheaths at his hips. Vek had never liked using a sword, and much preferred his forks.

So he'd barely had any time alone with Mia the evening before. He'd eaten the last meal of the day with her and the gladiators, sitting quietly, watching them all interact with easy conversation and smiles. Every time someone had included him in the discussions, he'd had to fight off his surprise. Thankfully, the Earth women did most of the talking.

Long after the House of Galen had fallen still and silent, Vek had snuck out of his cell and gone to Mia's room. She'd been curled into a tight ball in the middle of her big bed. He'd sat beside it and watched her sleeping. He'd fallen asleep against the wall, his sleep undisturbed by nightmares and filled with dreams of Mia.

He lifted his gaze to the distant horizon. Heat shimmered off the sand, but ahead, he spotted the long, dark silhouette of the Illusion Mountains. Corsair was in the lead with Galen. While the imperator rode one of the dark-scaled *tarnids*, the caravan master rode a different animal. It had a powerful body, a long neck, and ran on two legs. It was covered in beige scales, and was faster and more maneuverable than the *tarnids*.

Harper rode beside Mia, with Raiden and Thorin behind them. Two of Corsair's caravan workers followed at the rear, their *tarnids* loaded with packs, tents, and water pouches. Galen had decided to keep the group smaller, much to the complaints of the other gladiators. He'd left Saff and Blaine in charge of the House of Galen, and told the unhappy Nero and Lore they were in charge of training the lower-level gladiators and recruits in his absence.

Vek fell back beside Mia. "Have you drunk some water?"

She rolled her eyes at him. "You asked me that like ten minutes ago. I'm fine."

"You should snack as well, to keep your energy up."

"I'm not the one running instead of riding."

"I am not hopping on that...animal."

Mia's *tarnid* snuffled out a disgruntled breath, almost as though it agreed with him.

Another hour passed, and Vek persuaded Mia to sip some water and eat some travel snacks. He watched her carefully. He did not want her dehydrated.

Ahead, Corsair pulled his beast to a halt, and pointed forward. "There."

Vek scanned the desert and spotted it. The sand looked like it had been churned up and disturbed. A bad smell hit him. A burning stench, mixed with the scent of rotting meat.

The Gargas Badlands.

When they reached the edge of the Badlands, everyone dismounted. The men began to pull on large packs, while Corsair's workers corralled the *tarnids*.

Vek pulled a pack onto his back, tightening the straps. The weight didn't bother him, but he didn't like the constrictive feel of it. Mia and Harper both carried smaller packs.

"Everyone follow my steps," Corsair called out. "I know my way through the Badlands. Keep your voices low, so we don't disturb the death borers below. One wrong move, and you'll wake them all up."

They went single file, following behind the caravan master. Vek stayed behind Mia, in the center of the group. They all walked carefully, gently setting their boots down wherever Corsair indicated.

The ground was rough. In parts, it was sandy, and in other parts, rocky. Narrow paths twisted up and over rocks, and passed deep gashes that opened up in the sand. The stench of something burning was strong from the crevasses.

"This matches my idea of hell," Mia murmured.

"Hell?" Vek asked.

"A hot, terrible place where some humans believe bad people go after they die."

Vek made a sound. "To me, the fight rings were hell."

She glanced back at him. "No argument from me."

They were about a quarter of the way through the rough terrain, when suddenly Vek felt the ground start vibrating.

"Stop!" Corsair held up a hand. "Stay still."

Vek heard a trickle of rocks and sand falling, and he peered over the edge into a gully. Suddenly, a horrific creature burst up out of the sand.

Mia gasped and Vek wrapped an arm around her.

Everyone in the group froze, and Vek heard Thorin mutter a low curse.

The creature reared out, the top half of it flopping on the sand nearby and wriggling. It had a powerful, worm-like body in a mottled brown. It had no eyes, and its large mouth was ringed by huge fangs and two large, sharp pincers that opened out wide.

"They can detect vibrations," Corsair murmured. "Stay still."

The creature wiggled around for a little while longer, and then it burrowed back into the sand.

Vek did not like this place.

After what felt like an eternity, Corsair waved them on. They reached a large scar in the ground that cut across their path. Vek arched his neck and looked down into the giant crevasse. Far below, he saw a faint, red glow.

Corsair backed up a step, then ran and leaped across the fissure. He landed agilely on the other side.

One by one, the gladiators followed.

Mia stood at the edge, her hands clenched together. "Damn, that's a long way down."

Vek scooped her into his arms. She made a small, startled sound and wrapped her arms around his neck. He backed up a few steps and then ran at the chasm.

"Vek!" Her arms tightened.

He jumped into the air, flying across the deep crevasse. Mia made a strangled sound, holding him in a death grip.

He landed on the other side with a bend of his knees.

"Thanks," she said with a shaky smile.

He set her down. "I would carry you anywhere you want to go."

Her face softened. "Sometimes I wonder what I did to deserve you."

"All you have to do is be you."

They kept moving. Vek glanced back to where they'd come, and guessed that they were over half way through the Badlands.

"Almost there," Corsair said. "Keep moving."

Without warning, a death borer shot up out of the dirt right beside them, spraying sand and gravel over them. Mia screamed and Vek slammed his hand over her mouth.

The gladiators all jerked back. This death borer was smaller and thinner than the other. A juvenile, Vek guessed. It flopped around, searching, and Thorin and Raiden dodged back out of its way. Harper dropped to one knee, watching cautiously.

The death borer continued to squirm, impossibly close to the gladiators.

"Stay still," Corsair said quietly.

The death borer grazed Raiden, and one of its fangs snagged on Raiden's scabbard.

It moved, pulling the gladiator closer to its giant mouth.

Raiden lost his balance, but his face wasn't panicked. He threw his arms forward, ready to grab the rocky edge.

"Raiden!" Harper drew her own sword, and in a swift move, she swung her arm.

She sliced through Raiden's leather belt, cutting his scabbard away, and freeing him from the beast.

Raiden jumped and spun. He reached out, grabbing the hilt of his sword. He yanked his sword free as the death borer dropped back into the sand, taking Raiden's belt and scabbard with it.

"Drak." The gladiator pressed his hands to his thighs and sucked in a deep breath. Harper pressed into him. Everyone let out a collective breath.

"Wait." The group went silent again. Corsair held his hands out, studying the ground.

Everything was still and quiet.

The ground began to shake, far worse than before. All around them, pebbles bounced and danced on top of the sand.

"The borers are waking up!" Corsair yelled. "Run! Get out of here."

Adrenaline charged through Vek. He had to get Mia to safety.

He grabbed her hand and pulled her forward. They all ran, leaping over rocks and gullies. No one was worried about staying quiet or keeping to the path any longer.

"Move it." Galen waved an arm and leaped over a patch of pockmarked ground, his black cloak flaring out behind him.

Vek kept Mia close. Her face was pale and her attention was on the ground, to keep from tripping. He leaped over a large crack, pulling her with him.

The path narrowed between two large crevasses.

"Go." He urged her ahead of him.

She ran nimbly. He glanced back and watched as a patch of the Badlands collapsed behind them.

Then Mia screamed.

He spun back, blood spiking, and saw a large death borer rear up in front of Mia. Sand sprayed over them both.

Vek yanked out his fighting forks. "Down."

Mia dropped instantly, and Vek leaped over her. He thrust his forks forward, and jammed them into the creature's fleshy body.

The beast wriggled like mad, making a squealing sound. It dropped back down into the ground.

"Keep going," he ordered Mia.

She jumped to her feet and they rushed on. Ahead, Vek spotted the smooth stretch of sand that signaled the end of the Badlands. They were almost there.

Corsair reached the other side first, and swiveled. He pulled out a dangerous-looking crossbow and started shooting back at the death borers. High-pitched squeals echoed around them.

Suddenly, another creature reared up in front of Vek and Mia. It fell toward Mia. Vek wrapped an arm around her and lifted her off her feet. He dodged to the side, his feet touching the very edge of a deep crevasse. He jumped, landed on a pillar of rock, and set Mia down. He spun and stabbed the creature. It writhed wildly and dropped away.

His forks were slick with blood, and he heaved in a breath. He turned back to Mia. "Are you okay?"

She nodded, then she looked over his shoulder and her eyes widened. "Vek!"

Sharp teeth sank into his back with a spike of pain. He was yanked backward, off his feet.

The death borer pulled him into a shallow gully. He gritted his teeth and craned his neck. The creature was dragging him to a large crack at the bottom of the depression. He tried to hit the borer with his forks, but couldn't reach it to make contact. He shoved the weapons in his sheaths and reached out, trying to grab the passing rocks. He felt his skin tearing off his fingers, but he managed to grab on to a ledge. His muscles strained as he held on. The animal kept wriggling, tearing at his back. Blood slid down his skin in a wet smear.

"Vek!" Mia's face appeared above him. She was on her belly, leaning over the edge. She reached out and managed to grab one of Vek's wrists. But he knew she wasn't strong enough to pull him up.

"Mia. Do not risk yourself."

"You would for me!"

"Let me go."

"No," she said fiercely. She slid a hand down her side and a moment later, she aimed a pistol over Vek's head. She fired. And again. The noise was deafening to Vek's sensitive hearing.

She made a sobbing sound and fired again. The borer squealed, and he felt it release him.

Mia shoved the pistol away, and gripped both of Vek's wrists. She tried to heave him up, her face set with grim determination. He pushed his feet against the rocks and thrust upward. Working together, they pulled his body over the edge. He sprawled on the hot sand, panting.

"Vek. Oh, God." Mia crouched beside him, her hand

running over his hair. "I thought I'd lost you. Oh, your back!"

Vek pulled in a shuddering breath, and blocked out the pain. He sat up and yanked Mia into his arms. He held on tight. "It will heal. Thank you, Mia."

She hugged him back. "You're mine to protect, too, babe."

MIA FELT like she'd been walking for hours. She was hot, tired, and dusty. So very, very dusty.

She looked over at Vek. He was two steps ahead of her and she had a perfect view of his back through his torn shirt.

Her stomach turned over. It was so torn up. She'd cleaned it, and his torn-up hands, and spread med gel over them. The ugly wound from the death borer's fangs was healing, but it still made her heart clench. Vek had already suffered so much, and she hated him being hurt saving her.

The death borers would haunt her dreams for a long time to come.

The Badlands were thankfully behind them, and they were now in the rocky foothills of the Illusion Mountains. The mountain peaks reared up above them—sharp, jagged spikes that made her think of monsters' fangs. There was no vegetation, and everything around them was a beige color.

She noticed that Vek seemed tense. Suddenly, he

went still and crouched. He touched the ground and sniffed.

"What is it?" she asked.

"The scent of the Neralla flower is growing." He shook his head. "It's much stronger now."

She watched him carefully. She hoped to hell the Neralla scent couldn't affect him like it had when the Nerium had injected it in him.

They moved on, Vek moving up beside Corsair in the lead. Mia prayed they were headed in the right direction. She looked up at the peaks again. She hoped that Dayna, Ryan, and this other survivor were close by.

Stay strong. We're going to get you out of here.

She watched Vek prowl ahead, making a low growling sound in his throat. Mia frowned.

"Are you okay?" she asked.

A single, curt nod. "I do not like this place."

There was a little vegetation now—stubby, spiky plants suited to the climate. As they climbed higher, the sunlight started to wane, and the temperature thankfully dropped from scorching to bearable. The shadows deepened around them, and Vek grew more agitated.

"We need to set up camp," Corsair called out. "It'll be dark soon, and we don't want to be roaming the mountains at night."

"Any predators we should know about?" Galen asked.

"Nothing that I know of. But the mountains themselves are disorienting in the light, let alone the dark. A person wandering around is likely to end up at the bottom of a ravine."

Vek was wandering ahead. He stopped and pointed. "Caves."

The openings were farther up the slopes. There were several dark, yawning mouths, looking like the gaping maws of monsters.

"We have our tents," Corsair said. "Unless we get hit with a storm, I suggest we don't risk running into any unfriendly wildlife."

The gladiators set to work, setting up the tents. They were plain, circular affairs, just tall enough for a man to stand up inside of them.

Mia helped Vek set his tent up a little away from the others. She knew he wouldn't sleep, if he was surrounded by lots of people. Raiden and Thorin lit a small fire and Galen disappeared into the shadows. He came back in minutes with a lizard-like animal.

Corsair nodded. "An *ashen*. Good eating."

Before long, the creature was roasting over the flames. Mia sat down, listening to the quiet murmurs of the gladiators. Vek appeared, choosing the choicest pieces of meat for her plate. He seemed determined to feed her, much to the amusement of the others. But he didn't join them. Instead, he prowled the edge of the camp. Restless.

"Is he okay?" Harper asked.

Mia frowned. "He was, but now that we've reached the mountains, he seems...off."

"Maybe his injury from the death borer is bothering him?"

"I don't think so. It's almost healed." She watched as he vanished into the darkness.

"You care about him."

Mia looked at the other woman. "You fell in love with your alien. Vek can be a little wild, and looks different with his blue skin, but he's no less loyal or protective than Raiden. Beneath all of his...alienness is a man. A protective, loyal man. And I know he cares about me."

Harper smiled. "Believe me, after everything we've been through, if you can find someone who protects you, cares for you...even if he's blue...you hold on. You hold tight."

"He's suffered so much," Mia murmured.

"Make sure what you feel isn't sympathy, Mia. Because if you go there with Vek, something tells me he won't ever go back." Harper looked into the night shadows. "That once he claims you, you'll be his forever."

"I know." Excitement, fear, hope, and a number of other emotions whirled around inside of Mia. She'd never been in love, never felt that anyone would put her first. No one had ever made her feel special...except Vek. God, she wished she had one of her journals so she could write down the lyrics bursting inside her.

She made up a plate of the meat and headed to find Vek. She found him standing at the edge of the camp, staring out into the darkness.

"I brought some dinner for you."

He turned and took the plate. "Thank you." His voice was low and raspy. She watched as he wolfed it down.

"More," he said.

Mia guessed he'd expended a lot of energy running through the desert today. She went back to the fire, and loaded up another plate. He devoured the food again, shoveling it into his mouth.

She watched him with a frown. Something was wrong. Vek was usually a careful eater. She reached up and touched his face. His skin was molten hot. "You're burning up!"

"Fine," he growled.

He wasn't even speaking in full sentences anymore. She peered into his face, and suddenly he swept an arm around her. The empty plate dropped to the ground as he pulled her in close.

Heat pumped off him, and she could see his corded muscles straining under his skin. "Vek—"

His mouth slammed down on hers, strong and unyielding.

The power of the kiss forced her head back. Her heart was pumping hard, but she wasn't afraid. She slid her hands into his hair and kissed him back. This was Vek. Everything about him sang to something in her blood.

But as he took control of the kiss, his tongue plunging into her mouth, she realized that tonight he was more aggressive, more out of control.

Suddenly, he pulled back, and Mia swayed on her feet. He stared at her with that burning gaze, then he growled and prowled back into the darkness.

Mia wrapped her arms around herself. She hurried over to Galen. He was seated on a rock, his long legs stretched out in front of him.

"Something's wrong with Vek. He's agitated, amped up."

Galen frowned. "It's been a tiring day—"

All of a sudden, a roar echoed through the night. *Vek.*

Galen shot to his feet, and Mia spun. She ran toward the sound, conscious of the others right behind her.

Vek's shape appeared in the darkness. He was on his knees, his head thrown back.

She skidded to a halt beside him. "Vek, what's wrong?"

"I can smell the Neralla. So. Strong."

God, it was affecting him. Was the scent powerful enough to impact him the way it had when he'd been injected?

"So hot." A groan ripped from him. His eyes looked like liquid gold as they locked on her. "Mia. I want Mia."

There was hot possession in his words. Her gaze dropped down of its own accord and she saw the hard bulge at the front of his desert trousers. Her mouth dropped open.

Vek threw his arms out and roared again.

"Drak." Thorin pushed forward, shaking his head. "I recognize this."

"What?" Mia spun to face the big gladiator. "What's wrong with him?"

Thorin stared down at her, with a hard look on his face. "He's going into a mating frenzy."

CHAPTER NINE

"Into a what?" Mia felt like her heart had stopped beating. She watched Vek leap up and prowl around in circles.

He shot her a look that melted her bones. "Won't... hurt you." He sprinted away, moving agilely over the rocks. He headed toward the mouth of the closest cave.

He disappeared inside, and a second later, a roar echoed from the confines of the cave.

The sound was so angry, so alone, so afraid. Mia pressed her clenched fist to her aching chest.

"A mating frenzy," Thorin said. "It happens to certain species that have more primal animal instincts. It usually hits at specific times through their life, but it's different for every species."

"What triggered this?" she asked.

"The scent of the Neralla, maybe?" Thorin answered, his gaze heavy on Mia. "Or the presence of his mate. The one person who ignites his beast within. I don't know enough about his species to be sure."

Regan had told Mia that Thorin's beast rose to the surface at times. He clearly knew what he was talking about.

"What's going to happen?" Mia asked.

A muscle ticked in Thorin's strong jaw. "It's going to get worse. His body will be on fire, and without some release..."

Mia's heart knocked hard against her ribs. She grabbed the gladiator's arm. "What?"

"Most likely, he'll slip into a coma."

She gasped. *No.*

Galen cursed, running a hand through his dark hair.

Mia swallowed, realization dawning. "So he needs...sex?"

Thorin nodded. "And a lot of it. Usually a mating frenzy lasts for several hours."

"What if we contain him?" Galen suggested. "Sedate him?"

Thorin shook his head. "The overload of hormones in his body needs to be purged. He'd still end up slipping into the coma."

"A coma?" Mia repeated in disbelief. She pressed her hands together, terrified for Vek.

"And he'll be in agony until that happens," Thorin finished, a sympathetic look in his eyes.

Mia straightened, her thoughts racing. "I'm going in."

Galen stepped in front of her, blocking her way. "Mia."

Harper joined the imperator. "Mia, you don't have to do this."

"He could hurt you," Galen continued.

Mia shook her head fiercely. "Vek would *never* hurt me. He's mine." A sense of rightness filled her. He needed her help. No one in her life had ever really needed her. Her family were all composed, smart, and highly competent. None of them had ever asked her for help or needed her to do anything for them.

Galen looked into her face, that one, ice-blue eye staring at her like he could see right through her.

"Harper, grab Mia and Vek's gear, and take it up to the cave. I doubt that Vek will tolerate a male near him or Mia right now."

Mia gave Galen a shaky smile. "Thank you." She set her shoulders back and walked up to the cave entrance.

She stood there for a second, hesitating, and another deep roar echoed from inside. *Oh, Vek.*

Harper appeared, dumping blankets, pillows, and packs at Mia's feet. She cleared her throat. "Mia, you don't—"

"It'll be fine." She looked at her friend. "If it was your man in there, what would you do?"

She saw the answer in the woman's eyes. Harper had fallen in love with Raiden, and Mia knew the woman would do anything to save the man she loved.

"Vek saved me. He stood up for me. But I won't pretend this is all about him," Mia admitted quietly.

Understanding echoed on Harper's face. The woman reached out and gave Mia a tight hug. "You're hiding a gladiator's courage in that small body."

"I'm making this up as I go. I just know I'm not abandoning him."

As Harper left, Mia turned, blocking everything out except Vek. She crouched and scooped all the gear into her arms and stepped into the cave.

Inside was nearly pitch black. She set the blankets and pillows down on one side, and then reached into a pack and felt around until she pulled out a small travel lantern. She touched a button and a golden glow filled the space. It didn't illuminate the entire cave and she stared into the darkness at the back of the cavern.

She wondered how far back it went. And where was Vek?

She heard a low growl.

The sound raised the hairs on the back of her neck, but Mia pressed her lips together and made herself walk forward.

Vek needed her.

She pulled in a deep breath and reached up. She opened the buttons on her shirt and shrugged it off. Her breasts were so small that she hadn't bothered with any sort of bra or support. Then, she quickly undid the fastenings on her trousers and let them slide down her legs.

Wearing only her panties, she stepped forward. "Vek?"

There was a predatory silence. Heavy and weighted. She swallowed, her skin tightening. She knew something hungry was watching her from the darkness.

She saw a slide of something in the shadows, and

forced herself to stay still, even though some deep, old, instinctual part of her brain wanted her to run.

Then he stalked out of the darkness. His hot golden gaze on her.

He was naked. Her gaze was drawn to his large, muscled body. She took it all in—his ripped muscles, his strong arms, his powerful thighs. The huge cock that made her heart trip. He was wild, primal, fierce.

He came in close, and she smelled him—man and musk. He circled her, making low growling sounds in his throat. An electric tingle spread over her skin.

"Pretty," he drawled.

She trembled. As he crossed back in front of her, she saw that his markings were the darkest she'd ever seen them. A black the same color as deepest space.

He stepped up close, his chest brushing hers. He leaned down, and she felt his nose touch her cheek, then slide over her skin. He breathed her in, and she felt his breath panting against her skin.

Mia tilted her head back to give him better access. He growled and pulled her onto her tiptoes, his tongue licking along her neck. She shivered, spiky sensations racing through her. She went damp between her thighs. Then he scraped his teeth down her skin and she cried out.

"Mia." A guttural, hungry growl.

Sweet relief filled her. He knew who she was. "I'm here, Vek. For you."

He lifted his head, and his mouth landed on hers. His tongue swept into her mouth, devouring her. Like he wouldn't survive if he didn't get enough of her.

Vek let out an untamed growl, his big hands sliding up and down her back. Mia felt his thick cock brushing against her belly. She reached between them and circled her hands around it. God, he was so big. He groaned, rocking his hips against her. She stroked him, marveling at how hard he was.

"You like that?" she asked.

"Yes." His hips bucked against her touch.

She saw the veins and muscles straining under his blue skin. "Touch me, Vek."

His big hands cupped her breasts and she choked back a cry. Just one rough touch and her body was going up in flames.

Then he stepped back and slid a hand into her short hair, cradling her skull in his big palm. "Mia." A strained sound. "Can I have you?"

Everything in her, every cell, vibrated with need. With the sense of rightness that was growing stronger every second.

"You can have me, Vek. I'm all yours."

Another untamed growl. He dropped to his knees and then gripped her panties. With one violent flick of his wrist, they were torn off. As the silky fabric fluttered to the ground, his arms wrapped around her. He surged upright and lifted her into his arms. As he carried her over to the pile of blankets, she felt the brush of his cock against her thighs.

Mia's breaths were coming fast now, anticipation clawing at her.

Vek lowered her down and pushed her onto her back with a big palm pressed to her belly. He was staring at her, his gaze focused, and his chest heaving. He stroked his hands over her, touching her everywhere—her breasts, down her sides, across her belly, down her legs. He touched her like he was memorizing every part of her skin. Then he leaned down and pressed an opened-mouthed kiss to her belly. She writhed, her fingers sliding into his hair.

Then she felt his hand traveling up her thigh. His fingers delved between her legs, and she rocked against his touch.

She looked into his face and gasped. A set of fangs had descended in his mouth. His normal white teeth were still there, but there was also a pair of black, glistening fangs. They looked like they were made of obsidian.

"Vek?"

His lips parted, and she saw two golden drops of fluid form on the end of the fangs.

Before she could wonder what it was, he kissed her again. A glorious taste filled her mouth. *Oh. Oh, God.* Her belly contracted, desire racing through her. She still tasted Vek, but she realized the fluid mixed with her desire and enhanced it—like drinking a glass of exquisite wine.

She surged against his big body. "Vek, I need you."

He crouched over her, his gaze never leaving her face. Then he sat back, his hands circling around her thighs. He tugged her closer, making her gasp, until her legs were splayed over his hard thighs.

He paused, his gaze traveling over her, an unsure look on his face.

Mia reared up and brushed her fingers against his cheek. She had to remember that this was his first time. "Take me, Vek."

That was clearly enough to reassure him. He circled his cock and brought it between her thighs. She felt the broad head brush through her folds. *Oh, God.* She tensed, and reached out, her hands gripping the blankets beneath her.

Vek thrust inside her. She made a strangled sound, and felt the burning sting that accompanied his entry. She was stretched so far, she could barely stand it.

Any uncertainty he'd felt was gone. With a deep groan, he pushed forward, lodging himself deep inside her. He was following instinct now, and he started thrusting into her, over and over.

Mia's breasts bobbed with each thrust. She was pinned between the fabric beneath her and the hard man above her. He gripped her bottom, lifting her up to meet the hard drive of his cock. He was making a wild snarling sound that mingled with Mia's cries. Her body was alive with fierce need, a massive rush of sensation drowning her.

"Vek. Vek!"

He slammed relentlessly into her. She felt his muscles tensing, and knew his release was getting closer. He reared forward, his chest close to her, covered in a sheen of perspiration.

"Touch my clit," she panted.

He reached down, his thumb brushing the swollen nub between her legs. Pleasure crashed into her and she grabbed his shoulders, her nails sinking deep.

Mia's orgasm sucked her under, bigger and wilder than anything she'd experienced before. As she rode out her release, she watched Vek's body stiffen. He thrust deep one last time, buried to the root, and threw his head back.

As his release hit him, his roar echoed around the cave.

VEK SUCKED IN AIR. It brought him a hit of Mia's sweet scent, mixed with the muskier smell of sex.

Need was still riding him hard, flames that had been doused for a second rising again to lick his insides. For a moment, he'd felt sated with her sweet body.

Now he needed her again.

He looked down at her, and saw her eyes were closed. He froze. Had he hurt her? But then he saw her lips curve into a very pleased smile.

Her eyes fluttered open, and when she saw him, her smile widened.

Pride filled Vek. He'd given her pleasure. He could see that. He'd pleasured his mate well.

And for a blissful moment, he'd found a pleasure he'd never experienced before.

But now, he could feel the fire growing inside his gut again. He shifted off her, feeling unsettled. He pushed to his feet and paced across the rocky cave.

He hated being out of control. It reminded him too much of the drugs, of the Srinar, of being helpless.

"Vek, it's okay. You're in a mating frenzy."

He turned to look at her. She was sitting among the blankets, her legs tucked beneath her, her pretty breasts bare. His cock twitched.

"Mating frenzy?"

She nodded. "Apparently it's normal for some species, yours included. Thorin said it will wane...in a few hours."

Hours. Vek growled, his hands curling. He started pacing again. He couldn't withstand hours of this.

"You're...turned on again." Mia's gaze was on his hardening cock.

"I can't control it."

"So don't," she whispered.

"I will not hurt you, Mia." He'd been rough with her already, and he worried he'd get wilder and rougher yet.

"I'm tougher than I look, babe."

He shook his head. It was his duty to protect her, even from himself.

"I want this, too." She pushed up to her knees. "I had all my choices taken away from me for a long time. I choose this."

Vek gritted his teeth together, fighting the growing need.

As he watched her, she turned onto her hands and knees, her up-tilted ass pointed in his direction. He growled, his gaze moving over her smooth, pink buttocks. Blood thundered through him, his heart a fierce drumming in his chest.

All thoughts raced out of his head. All that was left was hunger. He strode across the space, and dropped to his knees behind her.

He shaped the globes of her ass, and Mia pushed into his touch. He kneaded her flesh, staring at the contrast of his big, blue hands against her smooth, creamy skin.

Mia made a mewling sound, and he slipped his hand between her thighs, stroking her folds. She was pink and swollen from taking his cock. He couldn't believe that her small body had accepted him. Before, when he'd taken her for the first time, he'd watched her body receive his big cock with amazement. It had felt so good. So tight and warm. He shuddered. He wanted to slide inside her again.

He leaned over her and stroked her spine. She was so seemingly delicate, his Mia, and yet she'd survived the Thraxians and the Srinar. She was fighting for her friends. And now, she was fighting for him.

Beneath her smooth skin, there was nothing delicate about her.

He lowered his head, and scraped his fangs over the nape of her neck. She pushed back against him, crying out again.

He smoothed the sting with his tongue, and then he moved his mouth down her back, kissing his way down along the knobs of her spine. Finally, he reached the pretty curve of her ass again. He kissed the soft flesh.

"Vek!"

He bit gently and she jerked.

"I need you inside me." She was looking back over her shoulder and he saw need blazing in her gaze. "Fuck me, please."

Her raw words were fuel to the flames. He gripped her hip with one hand and with the other, he brought his cock up. He paused to watch the big head pressed between her legs, then he surged forward.

"Yes!" She thrust back against him.

Vek started pounding into her, the sound of flesh slapping against flesh echoing in his ears. He felt her body clamping down on his cock, and he ground his teeth together.

"You're. Mine. Mia." He punctuated each word with a hard thrust.

He worked himself inside her, fucking her as hard as he could. The cave faded around him and there was only Mia, and her hot, tight body.

He felt her muscles tighten, saw her hands clenched on the cushions. She was getting close. He kept humping, pistoning inside her, driven by the vicious need within, and the hot pleasure of her body.

Suddenly, she stiffened and screamed. Her body clamped down on his cock so hard that Vek lost his rhythm, plunging into her with broken, uneven thrusts.

She shoved her ass against him, his cock so deep. Pleasure hit him, and he covered her with his body. He nudged her head to the side and sank his fangs into the curve of her neck.

It instantly threw her into another orgasm. As he filled her with his seed, his vision dimmed.

"Mia. *My* Mia."

CHAPTER TEN

Mia awoke to the feel of gentle licks on her inner thigh.

Her breath hitched and she looked down. Vek's dark head was between her legs. He was staring at her skin, a fascinated look on his face.

She shifted, small aches making themselves known. After the first two frenzied couplings, he'd taken her twice more. He lapped at her thigh, and she swallowed a moan. She hadn't thought her desire would still be this sharp. But as he kept licking, she felt a fiery tingle spreading through her body. Her belly clenched.

He looked up at her, his lips moving over her skin, then he focused down again. His mouth moved higher, licking her right between her legs. She moaned. His tongue delved inside her and she grabbed his hair, gripping hard.

"More." She made a strangled noise.

Vek kept lapping at her, then his tongue circled her

clit. She reared up against him. He pushed her back onto the blankets and kept licking at her like he couldn't get enough of her taste.

Then he sucked her clit into his mouth and Mia came, her back arching.

She flopped back onto the pillows, enjoying the little shivers that rippled through her as she came down from the high. Vek shifted to kissing her belly, then higher to the lower curve of her breast. As he moved across her body, she realized he was kissing her small bruises and the bite marks he'd left during their loving.

She smiled. Her wild, sexy alien was so strong and protective, but so sweet under all his muscles.

Finally, he moved up to lie beside her, like a big powerful cat. He stroked his hand down her body.

"Thank you, Mia."

"For what?"

"For giving yourself to me."

She leaned into him, nuzzling her face against his hard chest. "It was no hardship, Vek."

"You sacrificed—"

She rose up. "Nothing. There was no sacrifice involved. Of course, I wanted to help you, but if you think I didn't want this, you're crazy."

A small smile broke out on his face. "I do not know what I did to deserve you."

She cupped his cheek, enjoying the smooth skin with its faint hint of stubble. "I was fascinated by you the moment you stood up to protect me in the underground fight ring."

He wrapped his arm around her and pulled her back into the blankets.

She looked up at the ceiling of the cave. "Do you remember your homeworld? Your family?"

He released a breath. "Sometimes I get a hint of a memory, then it's gone. If I had a family, they never came for me."

His tone was emotionless, but she heard what he wasn't saying. "You don't know that. They might have searched for you. They might have fought for you." Her own family was devastated that Mia had no way home.

Vek stroked her hair. "All I remember is the fights. The stench of blood and sweat. The cold stone walls. Darkness. Knowing I'd have to kill."

"You are *never* going to fight to the death again," she said vehemently. "You're free."

His hands clenched in her hair. "I hope I never have to watch the life drain from another being's eyes." A deep breath. "I hope that I am never forced to fight for entertainment. I think...it would kill something inside me."

Mia tightened her arms around him, her ear pressed to his beating heart. It had a stronger, faster beat than her own. She wished she could take his past away, but all she could focus on was making sure his future was better. Making sure he had everything that he'd missed out on all his life.

And that included love.

God, she was falling in love with him. Mia let the idea settle, becoming a warm glow in her chest.

She was falling in love with Vek. She'd never been in

love before. Oh, when she was younger, she'd fancied herself in love with a couple of former boyfriends. But it had always faded. She was only just beginning to see that real love had depth. A foundation that so much could be built on.

Vek hadn't had love, either. Maybe they could learn about it together.

She stroked his chest. She'd tell him once they got back to Kor Magna. After this mating frenzy had passed, and they'd gotten Dayna, Ryan, and the other woman back safely.

Then there'd be time for just Mia and Vek.

He started shifting against her, restless, and a low growl rumbled through his chest. If she wasn't mistaken, it looked like the frenzy was heating up again.

He leaped to his feet, naked and magnificent. Mia would never get tired of looking at his powerful body. He prowled away from her.

Mia went up on her knees. "Vek?"

He spun, his eyes glowing.

"I'm right here," she said. "Whatever you want. Whatever you need."

"I've been rough with you."

She held out a hand. "Let me take care of you."

He edged closer, fighting his own needs. When he was close enough, Mia gripped his hips, her fingers digging into hard muscle. His cock was rising up toward his muscled stomach—big and thick. She leaned forward and licked the broad head.

An untamed growl ripped from his throat.

Pre-come slicked the end and she lapped at it. The salty taste of him filled her mouth. Smiling, Mia held onto him, and sucked his cock into her mouth. She pulled him closer, seeing his hands form hard fists at his sides.

His cock was too big for her to take it all, but she sucked in as much as she could. She was rewarded with his harsh growls.

She tilted her head back a little and watched him. His golden gaze was locked on her, the muscles in his neck stretched tight as he watched where her lips were stretched around his cock.

He grew thicker in her mouth, and she knew he was getting close. She felt his strong legs tremble, his hips bucking.

She pulled back. "Lie down, Vek."

His muscles flexed as he shifted that powerful body and lay back on the blankets. Mia climbed over him and straddled his hips.

She pressed her hands to his chest. All that primal power caged in his powerful body. She flicked her short nails over his nipples, then she lifted her hips up. She slid one hand down to grip the hard base of his cock and guided it between her legs.

When it brushed against her slickness, she moaned. Then she lowered herself down, taking him deep.

Vek growled, his hands clamping onto her hips. "Mia."

"It feels so good to be filled by you," she panted. She was a little sore, but the sting added a pleasurable discomfort to the sensations.

"Yes." His word was barely intelligible.

Once she readjusted to the size of him, she started rocking her hips, riding him. His hands flexed on her hips and he helped her, lifting her up and down. Then, he took one hand and reached up to touch one of those fascinating black fangs. He brought his finger to her nipple and rubbed a drop of that golden liquid into her skin.

Warmth bloomed, pleasure radiating from her breast.

"Oh." Her hips bucked against him.

Vek collected more of the fluid. This time, his hand drifted down and slid between her legs, his finger rubbing against her clit.

Sensations detonated like fireworks through her. "Oh, God." Mia moved faster, need and hunger writhing inside her.

He rubbed even more fluid on her, where her body was stretched tight around him. "Your body is squeezing my cock so tightly." His hips pumped up, like he needed more as well. She was riding him hard, and he was pounding into her.

"Mia," he growled.

"Vek!"

She broke apart, pleasure bursting through her like an explosion. She saw his face tighten, and at the same time, he roared his release. Their shared cries echoed off the rock walls.

Collapsing on him, she pulled in a shuddering breath, small waves of pleasure still running through her.

Vek buried his face in her neck. "Mia."

VEK'S EYES snapped open and, as he always did, he took that brief second to catalogue his surroundings.

Staring at the rock roof, his gut clenched. Then he slowly relaxed. Not the fight rings. He wasn't a prisoner.

The small, warm weight on top of him was the biggest reminder that he was free.

Mia was asleep, using him as a bed, her face tucked against his neck and her legs straddling him.

Morning light pierced the darkness from the mouth of the cave. Then he realized something else—the churning mass of driving need and hunger had ebbed. He released a breath. He felt like himself again.

Vek stroked his hand down Mia's back. And it was all thanks to this small woman.

His little savior. *His*. The echo of that claim had been etched in his soul.

She stirred and pressed a kiss to the bottom of his jaw. She lifted her head and he saw her sleepy gaze.

"Hi," she murmured. "You okay?"

"The frenzy has passed."

A smile broke out on her face. "I'm glad."

Vek slid a hand to her hair and brought her lips to his. This kiss was slower, and he took his time to taste her. She made a purring sound in her chest.

With a nip to her bottom lip, he lifted his mouth from hers. "You should never have come in here. I could've hurt you."

Mia rolled her eyes. "You're welcome."

He tugged until her forehead pressed against his. "Mia." His Mia.

She opened her mouth to say something, but Vek cupped her ass with one hand, and shifted her. He rolled her, sliding his cock inside her with one firm, steady thrust.

A sound tore from her throat. "I...thought the frenzy had passed."

"It has." But he needed her. Just Vek and Mia, without the overriding need of the frenzy. He stilled. "Are you sore? Can you take me?"

Her cheeks pinkened. "Um, not too sore. That golden fluid that you, um, rubbed all over me...it seems to have eased some of the discomfort."

Vek ran his tongue over his teeth. The strange fangs were gone, and he figured they, and the fluid they produced, would only be present for the frenzy. He started slow, steady thrusts into Mia's tight warmth.

Her eyelids fluttered, her hands reaching up to sink into his biceps. Mia was no passive lover. She writhed beneath him, urging him on with quiet whispers and the lift of her hips.

Need rose in him, strong and overpowering. Mia's legs wrapped around his waist, and her hands shifted. He felt her heels digging into his back, and her nails sinking into his skin.

"More. Harder." Urgent cries. "I'm coming!" Her body started to shake.

He watched her release hit her, her mouth opening and her eyes locked with his. With his cock lodged deep inside, making them one, he watched every emotion cross her face.

With satisfaction riding him hard, Vek thrust one last time. Pleasure was a hard, hot ball at the base of his spine. As it splintered outward, his groan was deep and loud.

He turned to the side, keeping Mia pulled into the curve of his body.

"Wow," she murmured. "That was just as awesome as the wild monkey sex."

Monkey sex? Vek smiled against her hair. He loved Mia's Earth sayings that made no sense at all to him.

After the perspiration on their skin had cooled, she turned in his arms. She stroked his cheek. "We should head out and find the others. They'll be worried."

Vek nodded, reluctantly sitting up. He didn't want to let her go, but she was right. They needed to continue their mission.

She rose, her movements slow. She seemed as reluctant to leave as he was. He watched her find some clothes, and he didn't want that skin covered. He wanted her naked in his bed, and he wanted to stay cocooned with her.

But there were three women who were trapped and caged, fighting for their survival. Three women who needed their help. Vek would not leave them to their fate as slaves. He had to do his bit to help them, just as the people of the House of Galen and Mia had helped free him.

Mia went through her backpack, pulling out things. Together, they cleaned up and pulled on clean clothes. Pulling on his trousers, Vek felt the deep scratches on his back and ass. He smiled. Mia had claimed him just as surely as he'd claimed her. His only shirt was in tatters, so he shoved the remnants in his pack.

As they left the cave, he held her hand tightly. Stepping into the morning sunlight, Vek took a second to appreciate it, but then felt Mia fidgeting.

The others were all gathered around the remains of a fire. The tents were packed away, the gear all ready for travel. As Mia and Vek approached, Corsair and the gladiators all stood.

"You both seem fine," Galen said, his assessing gaze on them.

From beside him, Thorin snorted. "More than fine, I'd guess."

Harper pressed her tongue to her teeth, her gaze on Vek's back. "Those are some pretty deep scratches there, Vek."

Mia gasped and shifted to look at his back. Her eyes widened, heat in her cheeks.

He grabbed her hand. He loved wearing her marks. "The frenzy has passed."

"And Mia got to save you for a change," Harper added.

Mia tucked her hair back behind her ear. "It wasn't any great sacrifice."

There was laughter all around.

"Come and eat," Galen said.

Thorin grinned. "And I have a shirt you can wear."

Vek stared at the food cooking over the dying coals of the fire, and hunger exploded inside him. He suddenly realized he was starving.

But first, he needed to care for his mate. After pulling on his borrowed shirt, Vek loaded up a small plate with the most tender, succulent morsels. He filled a second plate for himself, and then sat beside Mia.

She stared at the pile of food with wide eyes. Vek picked up one piece and pressed it to her lips. "Eat. You need to refuel."

She chewed and Vek took his time feeding her.

Harper sat down beside Mia and lowered her voice. "Some of the screaming had us worried."

"God." Mia pressed her hands to her flaming cheeks. "I'm fine. I'm glad I'm not riding a *tarnid* today, but other than that, I'm fine."

Harper looked like she was fighting a smile. "I have some med gel, if you need it."

Mia looked at Vek, smiled, then turned back to Harper. "I'm good. Really good."

They finished eating, and finally, Corsair stood. "All right, time to pack up and move out."

The gladiators worked well as a team, getting the last of the gear stowed and loaded into the packs. Soon, their group was striding up the mountain path, heading deeper into the Illusion Mountains.

Vek stayed close to Mia, walking near Corsair as they followed a narrow track. The suns were rising. It would be hot today.

"How is the scent of the Neralla?" Corsair asked.

"Getting stronger. I am certain we are headed in the right direction."

They kept moving, the ground becoming rockier.

"Look," Corsair called out.

Vek looked over, and saw a Neralla flower growing out of a crack in a rock. Its petals were pretty, twinkling in the light.

"How can it grow there?" Mia asked. "There's no soil."

"Keep moving," Galen ordered.

Vek could move faster, but he kept himself at Mia's speed. More Neralla flowers dotted the ground, here and there. They had to be getting close.

They rounded the crest of a hill, and ahead was a narrow valley. Suddenly, Mia stumbled to a stop. "Holy hell."

Vek followed her gaze across the valley to the next jagged peak. He blinked.

On the next mountain top, he saw a giant structure nestled among the rocks. He'd never seen anything like it. It was made of metal, but dominated by a huge glass dome in the center.

"Drak," Raiden said. "That's the wreck of a spaceship."

"A crashed spaceship," Harper said. "It looks ancient."

Vek frowned. He had no experience with spaceships, but since he'd been freed, he'd seen some roar overhead in Kor Magna. This wreck was long, and from what he could tell, the huge dome would have been in the center of the ship.

"How is that dome intact?" Mia asked.

Vek stared at it, aware his vision was better than the others. "I can see something in the dome."

"What is it?" Galen demanded.

His gaze touched Mia's. "The dome is filled with green vegetation."

CHAPTER ELEVEN

As they hiked closer, Mia stared up with wonder at the crashed ship.

Some parts of it were long gone—twisted metal consumed by rock and dirt. But the giant glass dome towered upward, seemingly untouched by time.

As they trekked closer, Mia could now see the vines, trees, and plants inside. Most were deep green, but she also saw some splashes of pink, purple, blue, and yellow.

They climbed up the hill directly below the ship. Mia gasped. Ahead, Neralla flowers blanketed the ground.

Vek crouched and sniffed. "These are blocking my senses, but I think I can detect a faint trace of Dayna."

Mia's heart leaped. She'd missed Dayna so much, and to get her friend back safely would mean everything to her. *Please, they had to be close.*

Corsair scanned their surroundings. "No guards or any sort of security system that I can see."

"They probably don't need it out here," Raiden said.

Galen was frowning. "If they have fights or hunts out here, they couldn't get spectators here very easily. It doesn't make sense."

"Let's get closer," Corsair said, pulling a large knife from his belt. A blue-green electrical glow lit up the long blade. "Keep it quiet."

Finally, they reached the dome. It looked like a bubble, the glass more clouded at the bottom. The suckers and leaves of a giant plant were pressed to the surface.

"How do we get in?" Thorin said with a frown.

"We'll find a way." Corsair led them to the left.

They skirted around the dome, the gladiators searching the glass for any sign of a door or entrance.

There was nothing.

They stopped, the men formulating ideas of what to try next. Out of curiosity, Mia reached out to touch the glass...and her hand passed straight through it like it wasn't even there.

"What the hell?" She snatched her hand back.

The others crowded around her. Vek, too, held out a hand and it passed through the glass.

Galen frowned. "I haven't seen anything like this before."

He clearly wasn't happy about it. Then, without a hitch in his stride, the imperator stepped through the glass and inside the dome.

Mia grabbed Vek's hand and tugged him forward.

Inside, a wall of humidity slapped her in the face. The interior of the dome was hot and sticky. The scent of lush plants and green growing things filled her senses. The plants grew thickly around them.

Corsair stepped inside, followed by the others. He crouched, fingering the mulch of rotting leaves on the ground.

Galen looked back at the glass of the dome and lifted his hand. This time, it didn't pass through. "Drak."

"We're trapped in here." Harper pressed both hands to the glass, pushing on it.

Beside her, Thorin did the same thing, straining as he exerted more force. "It's too strong to break."

Galen glanced around. "Let's find the women first, then we'll find a way out. Leave the gear here." He looked at Vek. "Which way?"

Vek sniffed and turned his head. "I can smell the faintest hint of Dayna's scent. That way."

Directly toward the center of the dome. Corsair nodded, shrugging off his pack. Then he pushed some branches aside, ducking beneath them. Mia passed through the branches, leaves brushing her skin. It felt as though they'd stepped into a rich, lush rainforest. Gorgeous flowers in every hue bloomed everywhere. She reached out to touch a plant with huge leaves the size of her body. When she made contact with one, the leaf curled in on itself.

"Look." Raiden had stopped, looking at a single red flower growing in a small clearing.

Galen put his hands on his hips. "An *oria*."

Mia looked at the pretty bloom. It had three blood-red petals edged with white, and it smelled divine. "What is it?"

"A very rare flower," Harper said. "Regan found one in the House of Galen and brought it back to life."

"It is a flower of the Creators," Galen said. "The advanced beings who seeded sentient life throughout the galaxy."

Vek leaned down and picked the flower. As one, the gladiators hissed in sharp breaths.

"Do you know how much that thing is worth?" Thorin said.

Vek turned and offered it to Mia.

She smiled. "Thank you." She tucked it in the top pocket of her shirt.

"Come on." Corsair waved them on.

They found a small path that wove through the trees. They moved in single file along it, pushing through the vegetation. They passed a tree with huge, sprawling branches forming a canopy above them. It reminded Mia of an umbrella. Vines dangled down, and the branches were all covered in small puffs of gossamer-like flowers.

As they moved beneath the tree, she saw some of the flowers release, floating through the air around them.

"I'm a man of the sand, but this place is incredible." Corsair stopped and reached out to touch the trunk of the tree. The vines hanging nearby suddenly moved, snapping out to slap his wrist. "Ow." He yanked his hand back.

"Watch yourselves," Galen warned. "I don't like this place. None of these plants are native to Carthago. We don't know anything about what they're capable of."

Corsair hefted his glowing blade and pushed on. Vek stayed close to Mia, keeping larger branches and vines out of her way. He kept lifting his head, sniffing, his brow creased.

She saw his muscles were strung tight. "What's wrong?" She stroked her hand down his arm.

"I can't scent anything. There are too many smells in here."

"It's okay. We'll search this entire place if we have to." She turned to look back behind them at the path they'd followed. Then she gasped loudly.

At the sound, everyone turned. The gladiators muttered curses.

The path was gone.

It was as though all the trees and plants behind them had shifted and covered up the trail.

Mia looked around. She couldn't see the tree with the large branches and gossamer flowers anywhere.

A muscle ticked in Galen's jaw. "We keep moving."

Vek pushed through some bushes and paused. Mia moved close to him and saw that ahead, the plants were all shades of blue. There were several with long blue leaves, others that looked like large, blue orbs.

"Vek?"

He moved forward and touched a large leaf, his gaze focused. He slipped into the vegetation and Mia gasped. He...disappeared. In the blue vegetation, he was totally camouflaged.

He reappeared and prowled back to Mia's side.

"These plants are...familiar." There was confusion in his voice.

Mia wondered if Vek's homeworld had blue vegetation.

"Everyone, take a quick rest and drink," Galen ordered.

Mia drank the water Vek passed her and tilted her head back, staring up at the glass dome overhead. The thing was enormous. She couldn't believe it had been part of a spaceship, or that it had survived a crash. They were getting very close to the center of the dome now.

They set off again and the blue vegetation morphed back to green with a few splashes of red and orange. Mia wiped her arm across her sweaty brow. It felt like it was getting hotter.

Suddenly, Vek stopped, and she bumped into his muscled back. She side-stepped around him and saw a giant tree rising up in the center of a clearing. Its large, gnarled branches were thicker than Mia's body. Giant, clear pods about the size of a large human were hanging off it.

"Wow," Harper murmured.

Mia moved closer to the tree, studying one of the pods. They were translucent and there was something inside of them.

She stared, and her heart thudded against her chest. She raced forward. Behind her, she heard Vek growl and his steps slapping on the thick grass as he followed her.

Mia stopped under one pod. She reached up, but Vek grabbed her wrist.

"Mia?"

"Look." Her voice was choked. "Look inside the pod." She sensed the others joining them.

She watched as Vek looked up and then went still. He growled.

"What the drak?" Galen stepped beneath the pod.

Inside the pod was a sleeping woman.

Her naked body was curled up in a ball, and Mia could see her face clearly. She had some Japanese heritage, and her dark hair was pressed up against the clear side of the pod.

It was Ryan.

VEK PULLED MIA BACK, and together they watched Raiden draw his sword. Thorin moved beneath the pod, pressing his hands to it. Galen went down on one knee and nodded at Raiden.

The gladiator took a few running steps, pressed a boot to Galen's raised knee and leaped into the air with a flare of his red cloak.

He sliced his sword through the top of the pod.

It fell, and Thorin caught it with a grunt. He gently lowered it to the ground.

Corsair crouched over it, and using his electro knife, he carefully split the pod open. Ryan slid out, her skin slick with clear fluid and her wet hair stuck to her head. She didn't wake up.

Galen pressed a finger to her neck. "She's alive."

Vek wrinkled his nose. "I smell something in the pod. A poison or drug."

"Vek, give me your shirt," Mia said.

He shrugged out of it and she crouched beside the naked woman. "Harper, can you help me get it on her?" After Ryan was clad in the too-large shirt, Mia turned her gaze toward the trees. "What the hell is this place?"

Suddenly, Thorin made a strangled sound, and dropped to his knees. He clawed at his throat with his hands.

"Thorin!" Raiden dropped down beside his friend in shock, but then the other gladiator lifted his hands to his own throat and started coughing.

Vek spun and saw that everyone in his group was doing the same thing. Harper collapsed on the ground, writhing. Corsair fell to the grass with a thud.

Pulse racing, Vek turned to Mia. He didn't feel any different. Whatever it was, wasn't affecting him.

"Vek—" Mia was reaching a hand out for him, her face flushed, and her other hand balled at her chest. She tumbled forward and he caught her before she hit the ground.

He lifted his head and saw Galen was the only one still standing. The imperator's teeth were gritted, and he was clearly fighting the effects. But then he fell to one knee, coughing violently.

Vek realized it had to be the tree. He scooped Mia up and carried her away from it. He set her down on a patch of grass.

He hated to leave her, but he knew the others needed him. He ran back, and leaned down and scooped up Harper. He threw the woman over his shoulder. Then he stooped down awkwardly, and grabbed Ryan. He managed to get her on his other shoulder. Carrying both women, he trotted back to Mia. He laid the women down beside her.

Raiden was next. The gladiator was solid muscle and heavy. By the time that Vek had moved the man out of range of the tree, he was sweating.

He carried Galen, and then went back for Corsair. That's when Vek noticed his skin was turning pink, obliterating the blue. It stung, and in places, his skin was blistering.

He grabbed the caravan master and turned. He forced his feet to move, pain coming alive inside him. His muscles were burning and his skin felt like it was on fire.

He placed Corsair beside Galen's motionless body, and went back for Thorin.

Grimly, Vek studied Thorin's large form. There was no way he'd be able to lift the man. Instead, he hooked his hands under Thorin's arms, and started dragging the gladiator. Vek gritted his teeth and heaved. Aches bloomed in him, and his skin was burning in agony.

It was only minutes, but it felt like days by the time he got Thorin back to the others. Vek collapsed down beside Mia, panting. Nausea rose, bile stinging his throat. He pushed it down, then reached out and stroked Mia's hair.

Her delicate eyelashes rested against her pale cheeks. He willed her to wake up.

Minutes ticked past, then he heard her breathing change. Behind him, he heard some of the gladiators stirring, but he stayed focused on his Mia. Her eyes flickered open.

"Vek?"

"Stay still." He stroked her cheek, and then heard someone retching.

"Your skin." She hissed. "It looks burned."

"It'll heal."

"Drakking hell," someone groaned.

Galen staggered to his feet. "What happened?"

"The tree," Vek said. "It released something that affected you all."

The imperator looked back toward the large tree, then back at Vek. "You carried us?"

Vek nodded.

Galen's single eye flashed. "Thank you."

Mia got to her knees, wavering a little. "How's Ryan? Did she wake up—"

Beneath them, the ground rumbled.

Vek crouched, his palm pressed to the grass. He felt the vibrations.

"What now?" Galen drew his sword.

"Something is...moving," Vek said.

Vines shot out of the ground. Dirt and grass sprayed into the air, and Mia screamed. Vek leaped to his feet and yanked out his forks. One vine wrapped around his forearm. He slashed at it with his other hand, the sharp edge of his fork slicing it away.

But before he could move, more vines rushed at him, wrapping around his ankles, and then his wrists. *No.* He let out a roar.

He was jerked into the air, his forks landing harmlessly on the ground.

He saw Mia struggling against the vines that had wrapped around her. Around them, the others were all constrained by the thick, green vines. He saw one vine slither around Mia's neck and tighten.

"Mia!" He struggled, but the vines held him in place.

Her eyes bulged and she fought, but slowly, her struggles turned sluggish. Helpless, all Vek could do was watch. He roared again. Whoever was responsible would die.

Mia slumped and instantly, he saw the vines loosen. She fell face first onto the grass. The rock that had lodged in his chest loosened. She was alive, just unconscious. He glanced around, and saw the others were all unconscious, as well.

Vek growled, straining against the plants. Then he heard a noise.

He lifted his head, and saw the bushes nearby rustling.

Someone was coming.

CHAPTER TWELVE

Mia stirred. Her head felt fuzzy and her nose was tingling. She grimaced, and felt grass prickling her cheek.

That's when she heard footsteps and the murmur of voices. It was followed by one of Vek's fierce growls.

She lay still, her cheek to the grass, and opened her eyes to slits.

She saw tall, green-skinned aliens emerge from the vegetation. Their skin was thick and cracked, almost like the bark of a tree. Their hair was brown, and resembled a tangle of tree roots.

The aliens stopped in front of Vek. Oh, God, he was hanging in the air, vines holding him tight. He was straining against them, snarling.

"Welcome, beast. We are the hunters."

The group of five aliens spoke in unison, their voices like the whisper of wind through branches.

Vek growled again.

"We are hired to secure only the best and most unique hunters for the tournament."

"Slavers," Vek ground out.

"We are the Nerium." Fierce whispers. "It is an honor to hunt. It is not slavery."

"We just want our women, and then we'll leave."

"No one leaves the tournament," the tallest alien said. More whispers, as the others murmured their agreement.

Vek struggled against the vines. One green alien stepped in close to him, examining him like he was livestock.

"I see why our clients wanted you. You are a prime specimen." The alien turned back to the others. "He will honor the hunt," they all said in unison.

"Clients?" Vek said.

"Yes. They wanted you back."

Mia sensed something and slowly moved her head. She saw that Galen was awake. The imperator was lying on the ground, watching the aliens. He shook his head at her and leaned over to wake Raiden.

"I will not hunt for you or your drakking clients," Vek spat. "I will not fight for someone's bloodthirsty pleasure."

The tall alien tilted his head. "Then your friends will die."

Mia froze. Vek gave a feral snarl.

"Who are your bloodthirsty clients?"

Another rustle of the bushes, and a sixth figure stepped out. Mia's stomach dropped. She recognized the man with the disfigured back, misshapen face, and huge tumor dominating his face. He was a Srinar.

Vek went wild, jerking on the vines and struggling.

"You will fight in the hunt, beast," the Srinar said. "Only then will I let your friends go unharmed."

Mia froze in horror. *No.* She realized that this was another type of fight ring. It might look nicer and smell nicer, but it was just the same as the subterranean, dirt-covered arena of the fight rings.

The Srinar had never stopped their ugly games. They'd come here, to these dangerous, desolate mountains and were forcing people to fight against the deadly plants, and whatever else was hiding in here.

All in the name of sport and money.

She would not let Vek suffer that again.

Mia surged up. "Let him go!"

One of the green aliens turned to look at her. She took a step toward them, and suddenly vines burst out from the alien's hand. They snaked around her body, and she tried to break free of them. Another one slithered up and shoved inside her mouth. A scream echoed in her head as she choked.

"Mia!" Vek was struggling wildly now, his gaze locked with hers.

She couldn't breathe!

"Choose, beast-man," the Srinar said, smiling.

The vine didn't budge, blocking Mia's airway. She jerked, trying to get air into her burning lungs.

The Srinar clasped his hands behind his back. "Fight and save your friends. Or do nothing, and she will be the first to die."

Mia shook her head vigorously, tears leaking out of the corner of her eyes.

Vek's chest heaved, all his muscles stark under his skin. His face was a fierce mask.

"Let her go. I will hunt and fight for you."

Pain speared through Mia's chest. But at Vek's words, the vines retracted. She heaved in air, and then the vines unraveled from her body.

She crashed to the ground, rubbing her sore throat. She looked up at Vek and their gazes locked.

No. His gaze was full of horrible, soul-shattering resignation.

VEK WATCHED as the Nerium rounded up the gladiators, herding them away. Mia fought and cursed, trying to reach Vek. Finally, Galen picked her up and, with a single, unfathomable look at Vek, the man turned to follow their captors.

Then he was alone in the small clearing. He heard the quiet whispers of the trees and the rustles of small, invisible animals in the undergrowth.

A long, mournful horn sounded through the dome.

He bowed his head. Once again, he stood in the center of a fight ring, waiting for his opponents to rip him apart. He lifted his arms, staring at his fighting forks and his hands. It seemed no matter how hard he tried, he would never be free.

He would always be dragged back to the darkness and blood.

The bushes to his right rustled, and suddenly a

monster bounded out. Vek lifted his forks and turned to meet it.

It was humanoid, but covered in thick, golden fur, with large claws and an elongated snout. Vek slashed out with his forks, and he saw the bright-green eyes in the creature's face. And the desperate horror reflected in them.

It knew this was a fight to the death.

Vek dodged, and then he felt the sting of claws across his side. He leaped back, and that was when he smelled it.

Neralla flower. Stronger than ever before.

The drakking Srinar were pumping it into the dome. He felt the fire start in his bloodstream, his aggression rising.

No. He let out a roar, trying to fight it. Memories struck him like arrows. Him, as a confused youngling, screaming as he was carried onto a ship...by a tall, green-skinned alien. The Nerium had kidnapped him.

He bellowed in rage. More memories came. Of the fight rings, of the drugs pumping into his veins. Of the swords prodding him into the ring, of the coppery tang of blood in his mouth.

His next roar turned his vision red. He spun, and saw fur and claws coming at him. He stabbed the creature. It let out a snarl, and he sank his hands into the fur. He spun, then tossed the beast.

It slammed into a tree trunk and fell to the ground, unmoving. Chest heaving, Vek wiped his forks on the grass, cleaning off the creature's green blood.

He stalked into the trees, listening for any prey. He

heard a buzzing noise and looked up. A small, metallic ball was floating in the air. It zipped behind a branch.

Vek bent his knees and leaped into the tree. He gripped a branch and shifted. He spotted the ball and snatched it out of the air. It made a beeping sound, the front of it moving to focus on him.

With an angry growl, he crunched the metal in his hand, and then dropped it to the grass. He jumped to the ground. Here, the grass was long, reaching to mid-thigh.

He wondered if the Srinar would keep his drakking word and free Mia and the others. *Mia.* Pain hit him. He would never again feel her smooth skin, taste her lips, or hear her cries beneath him. He closed his eyes. As long as she was alive and safe, that was all that mattered.

All of a sudden, the grass around him started swaying and making a swishing noise. Then, right before his eyes, it starting growing. It grew until it reached his waist, then his chest, then it reached his head.

Vek heard a rustle—quiet and stealthy. He turned his head, tracking the sound.

Another rustle on the other side of him, and he swiveled. *What was out there?*

Suddenly, a creature attacked, bursting out of the long grass. Vek got a glimpse of slashing, scythe-shaped claws, and a powerful body that moved on two strong legs balanced by a long tail. This creature was covered in bright feathers and let out a screech.

It smashed into him, and they slammed to the ground, crushing the long grass under their weight. Vek wrestled with it, feeling sharp claws slash at his belly. Blood slid down his skin.

With a growl, he heaved, rolling until he was on top. He landed a chop to the creature's powerful chest, stunning it, and then jumped up. Vek brought his foot down on the animal's neck, avoiding its snapping jaws.

He lifted his forks—

A heavy weight slammed into his back, knocking him off the creature. His arms got tangled in the long grass and he yanked hard to free himself.

Violent rage ignited in Vek. *His* kill.

Fight. Hurt. Kill.

A quiet part of him screamed. He'd never wanted to fight like this again. He reached over his shoulders and tore the attacker off him. He tossed the dark-skinned alien to the ground.

The humanoid man rose. He was well-muscled, with dark, striped skin and tattered fighting leathers. They stared at each other. The man's body was scarred, and there was no doubting that he was a fighter.

The tall grass around them laid flat in a circle. Like it was creating a make-shift arena. The clawed creature had escaped into the greenery.

"If you lose, you die. If you win, you lose," the man said in a raspy voice. "They will keep you here for years. Fighting, always fighting."

Vek tasted bile in his throat and stared at the man. It was clear this man had been here a long time. The Srinar must have had this place operating, along with the fight rings.

The man yanked a jagged silver blade off his belt. He charged at Vek with a roar.

Vek thrust his hands up, catching the man's sword in

his forks. They spun. The man ducked, drew back, then raced forward again.

They traded blows, ducking and weaving. Vek fell into fight mode, watching every move and step the man made. He'd become attuned to finding a fighter's weakness.

There. The way the man dropped his guard when he took a step back. Vek lunged and sank one of his forks into the man's belly.

The man staggered back, his blade falling from his grip. He stared down where Vek's weapon pierced his gut.

He lifted his face, and a calm, almost-peaceful look crossed his features. "Thank you."

The man fell to the ground and didn't move, staring up at the sky above, beyond the dome that was their prison. Vek dropped down beside him.

He gripped the man's shoulder and watched the life fade from the man's green eyes.

Vek lifted his head and roared out his despair. He'd never escape this. It was all he knew, all he was good at, and it was dragging him back.

He wouldn't drag Mia into this.

Mia would live.

Over the rustle of the leaves, he heard yipping and snarling getting closer. He rose to his feet, settling his grip on his forks.

A pack of huge hunting dogs burst out of the greenery and rushed toward him.

Vek held his weapons at his sides, waiting.

He would do what he always did. Fight. Survive.

He rushed in, swinging his forks. The dogs were covered in spikes, and fought as a pack. One leaped in to attack, clearly a diversion to keep him busy. The others moved to circle around him. He sank his fork into the lead dog and it cried out. Another dog leaped onto his back, claws slashing at his skin.

Vek shrugged it off, and as another rushed at him, he kicked it away. He ducked, swirled and swung, but as he fought, he felt himself tiring.

Hunt. Hurt. Kill.

The words pounded in his head with each beat of his heart. Mia's face drifted into his head.

Vek let out a pain-filled roar. He had a new motto now.

Save Mia.

He launched himself into the pack of hunting dogs.

CHAPTER THIRTEEN

One of the guards pushed Mia hard in the back and she stumbled. Raiden gripped her arm and kept her upright.

Her insides were churning, like she'd swallowed a deadly cocktail of acid. *Vek.* They had to help Vek.

Ahead, several tall trees speared up toward the roof of the dome. They had long, sturdy trunks, and thick, gnarled branches overhead. On the ground beneath the closest tree, she saw a large cage made of wood. The top of it was tied to ridged, twisted vines, thicker than her thigh.

The Nerium had disarmed the gladiators, and she watched two guards drop the swords, axes, and other weapons in a pile on the thick grass. In the distance, she heard Vek roar. She closed her eyes, the pain like a laser blast to her chest. She couldn't imagine how he felt, being forced to fight and kill again.

And he'd done it for her.

The guards shoved them all into the cage. It was barely tall enough for the gladiators to stand up in. Thorin had to hunch over.

The Nerium guards locked the door, and a second later, the cage lurched off the ground. Mia stumbled against Harper, and she heard low curses from the men.

They were pulled jerkily upward, until the cage was high in the trees. Mia gripped the bars and looked down. Their location gave them a perfect view of the vegetation below.

But then she turned her head and gasped.

"What the drak," Galen muttered.

The tops of the trees were filled with platforms, and wooden bridges linking them. It was a treetop city.

A number of Srinar and Nerium were walking along the platforms. Her lip curled. She recognized some large, horned Thraxian forms, as well. Anger exploded in her. All these fucking species who thought they had the right to enslave and hurt other people.

"What the hell is that?" Harper murmured.

Mia turned her head and saw where Harper was looking. On a large platform nearby, there were what looked like rows and rows of comp screens. Srinar manned each screen, watching intently, and occasionally tapping the screen.

An enraged roar filled the air, and Mia's heart clenched. She looked back at the ground, and caught a glimpse of Vek. He was whirling and jumping, fighting against a pack of giant alien dogs. She pressed a fist to her mouth. There were so many of them.

"They're streaming the hunts," a female voice said.

Mia swiveled. She saw that Ryan was awake, sitting on the floor of the cage with her back pressed to the bars.

"Hi, Ryan." Mia crouched beside the woman. "Are you okay?"

"I am now." Ryan grabbed Mia's hand and squeezed. "Thanks for coming—" Her voice broke, her lips trembled. "I've been alone for a really long time."

Mia wrapped her arms around Ryan, pulling her in for a hug. It made her realize how lucky she'd been to have Dayna and Winter, and now the other women, the gladiators, and Vek.

Oh, God. Vek.

Ryan looked up at the others, swiping tears from her eyes. "It's good to see all of you. I'm really sorry about this."

Galen crouched. "We'll get out of here. I am Galen."

"I know." Ryan's gaze slid over Galen's powerful form, before flicking up to Raiden, Thorin, and Corsair. "You guys pack an even bigger punch in real life."

The corner of Galen's mouth lifted, then his expression turned serious again. "Streaming?"

Ryan nodded. "From what I overheard when I first got here, they sell subscriptions for spectators to watch the hunts all over this part of the galaxy."

"Sand-sucking scum," Raiden bit out.

The imperator eyed Ryan. "Are you hurt?"

She shook her head. "Just a headache and a few bruises. They let me loose in the hunting grounds, but I didn't last long. Got nabbed by...something. Everything went black. That's all I remember."

"Have you seen Dayna?" Mia gripped the woman's arm.

Ryan shook her head. "I haven't seen anyone else from Earth."

"How the drak will we get out of here?" Thorin's big hands strained against the wooden bars. "Whatever the hell this wood is, it's too drakking strong to break."

As the gladiators huddled to discuss ideas for escaping, Mia looked back through the bars. When she'd been locked on the Thraxian ship, and then in the bowels of the underground fight rings, she'd missed trees, and flowers, and green. Now she looked out at the deadly playground below, and thought she'd be happy if she didn't see another tree for a very long time.

Suddenly, she saw Vek burst out of some bushes and into a clearing not far away. A cry strangled in her throat, and she wrapped her hands around the bars. Even from a distance, she could see that he was covered in blood. So much blood.

She watched him stab his forks into a hunting dog. She bit her lip hard, tasting blood in her mouth. He was doing the very thing that he'd told her would destroy his soul.

And he'd done it for her.

Mia looked back at the Srinar and their fucking screens. She'd already hated them, but the hate festering inside her now was an ugly, angry thing.

A flash of movement directly below them caught Mia's gaze. She shifted so she could look down. Someone had just run up one of the wooden ramps leading to the platforms. Mia tried to spot whoever it was, but they were moving fast and staying hidden.

She turned to look at the platform right beside the cage. Two Nerium silently stood guard. Suddenly, one of them was yanked backward and over the railing. He arrowed to the ground below, and landed with a *thump*. The second guard lifted his weapon, but was pulled around the other side of the large tree trunk. Mia heard the thud of something hitting flesh.

The gladiators stood, quiet and tense, watching and waiting.

A hooded figure appeared, and touched the lock of the cage. The door swung open.

Mia stared at their rescuer. The person wasn't very tall. Leather trousers covered lean legs, scarred, leather gauntlets peeked out from under a dark, rough, hooded cloak that kept their face hidden. Their savior was carrying a large, black bundle.

Galen moved forward. "Who are you?"

"No time for chit-chat. We need to move."

It was a *woman's* voice.

The woman dumped the bundle on the floor of the cage. It clanked as it hit, and when the woman kicked the edges of the blanket out, Mia spotted the gladiators' weapons.

Instantly, the men and Harper reached for their weapons. Suddenly, a Nerium guard rounded the trunk of the tree. As he spotted the open cage, his eyes widened.

The woman moved. Fast. She kicked the Nerium in the gut, and then whipped a wooden staff out of nowhere.

She swung the weapon with quick, vicious hits, her ragged cloak twisting around her body with each move.

The Nerium slumped to the platform with a groan, and the woman shifted her staff behind her back. She flicked her hood back.

Mia saw golden-brown skin, and long, black curls pulled back at the base of her neck. She had pale green eyes.

"You're human," Mia breathed.

"Yep." The woman relaxed her fight pose, moving her staff up against her shoulder.

"Who are you?" Harper lifted her swords from the pile, her gaze on the woman. "I don't recognize you from Fortuna Station."

"And you weren't on my ship," Mia added.

"I was on Fortuna. I was a cleaner." The woman cast a look at Harper. "Most people don't have any time for the people who scrub up the messes, so that's probably why you don't recognize me. Now, like I said, we need to move."

The woman disappeared along the platform. Galen and the others strode forward, and Mia hurried to follow her. The woman led them on a twisting path through the treetops. Once, they had to stop and crouch down, as Srinar passed by on an adjacent platform. Finally, the woman led them down a ramp and into the trees.

She didn't stop, following some path only she could see.

After a few moments, she stopped and pointed ahead. "You can get out that way. Go straight for another twenty meters, and you'll find a hidden door. Don't stop, don't turn. The plants will try to confuse you."

"Wait!" Mia said. "We aren't leaving. We have to get Vek."

The woman frowned. "The blue beast?"

Mia straightened. "He's not a beast. He's a man."

The woman raised a brow. "Sorry."

"And we have to find Dayna. She's another woman from Earth. We learned that there was another Earth woman here, and I guess that must have been you."

The woman's frown deepened. "There's no other woman here." She glanced over at Ryan. "Other than her. And she was just brought in a little while ago."

"How did you get here?" Corsair asked, studying her carefully.

"The Thraxians sold me to some desert traders. I escaped, but got nabbed by the Srinar."

Who *was* this woman? Mia blinked. She'd survived alone all this time? "What's your name?"

"On Fortuna, I went by Linda Taylor."

Harper nodded in recognition. "Lab cleaning crew."

The woman inclined her head. "But my real name is Neve. Now, I never saw her, but I did hear talk of another woman held here. They said she was a good fighter."

"That has to be Dayna," Mia said. "She was a former cop, and trained in martial arts."

"Wait." Harper held up a hand. "Hang on a second. You were on the space station under an assumed name. You were a cleaner, but you took down three aliens without breaking a sweat, and you hold that staff with a hell of a lot of experience."

"Was there a question in there somewhere?" Neve asked.

"Who the hell are you?"

"I work...or rather, worked, for Titan Corp."

Harper nodded slowly. "You were a corporate spy. Axis Corp spent a lot of money ensuring no one on Fortuna Station was there to steal secrets."

Mia's mouth dropped open. She knew corporate espionage between the companies going after the lucrative space market was fierce.

"Not enough, obviously." A small smile tipped Neve's lips, then it was gone. "I guess it doesn't really matter, now."

"What matters is that we all get out of here," Mia said. "Dayna? Any idea what happened to her?"

Neve shrugged. "She's not here now. Maybe she was killed."

Mia sucked in a breath, her chest going tight. *No.*

Harper touched Mia's shoulder, and Galen stepped forward.

"We'll worry about Dayna after," Galen said. "For now, we need to get to Vek."

Neve tilted her head. "If you go now, you'll get out safely. If you turn back...there is no guarantee the Srinar will ever let you leave this place alive."

Mia didn't wait for Galen to answer. "We aren't leaving without Vek."

VEK WAS TIRED. Pure rage was the only thing driving him now.

He swiveled and thrust out his weapons at an incoming alien fighter.

In his head, all he thought about was Mia. The thought of her kept him going. The thought of his time with her kept him swinging and dodging. It was the one special moment in his life that wasn't stained by blood and death.

He cut down another fighter.

Galen and the others would keep her safe. And she had her friends.

Their time together in the cave filled his head—her taste, her smell, the feel of her skin. The way she'd given herself to him completely.

It would be enough to sustain him until he found death.

He saw more of the small metallic balls whizzing through the air, circling each of the fighters. He stood over his last fallen opponent, chest heaving.

Ahead, the vegetation looked different. The lush green gave way to spiked, gray leaves that were long and narrow. They grew in clumps, reaching up as tall as Vek.

He approached carefully, one part of him listening for any incoming attackers. He knew he could track down other opponents, hunt them one by one using his skills and senses. But that would be giving his captors what they wanted. He would defend himself, but he wouldn't drakking hunt.

Suddenly, the gray plants started to move, and a gray substance began to ooze from the bottom of them. He stepped back, but it flowed quickly, covering his boots. He tried to lift his feet, but the goo was sticky and drying fast.

He was stuck.

An undulating war cry echoed through the trees.

Vek tensed and lifted his forks. He kept trying to move his feet, fighting against the hold of the plant's secretion.

Two orange-fur-covered aliens burst out of the bushes. One leaped at Vek, and he lifted his forks, stabbing at it. It yelped and flew over him.

The second one prowled by the edge of the sticky ooze, growling. Its eyes glowed with intelligence...and the will to live.

Abruptly, one of the spiky gray plants moved. The sharp edge turned into a blade, stabbing into the alien's leg, severing it.

The alien fell, its piercing wail filling the air.

Vek strained more forcefully against the ooze, and managed to get one foot free.

The gray plants moved again, one of those wicked spikes whipping around and rushing at him. He sliced out with his forks, cutting the spiky end off.

He freed his other boot and jumped onto the grass. He took one step, and saw another pointed spine racing at him. Fast.

Too fast for him to avoid.

It rammed into his gut, blood spraying. Agony ripped through his stomach. Vek looked down, and saw the branch had pierced him deep. More gray ooze flooded around him. It covered his boots, and then he saw it shift and start to run up his legs. Through the pain, he tried to kick it off.

It reached his knees, and now he felt it burning, eating through his leathers.

More wild, undulating cries echoed from ahead of him. He tried to move but the pain made him groan. The plant was holding him in place so the incoming fighters could tear him apart.

Vek let his fighting forks fall to the ground.

He wouldn't give the Srinar the chance to see him struggling, to see his feral despair. In his head, he saw Mia's face, and a sense of peace drifted over him.

The gray plant discharge reached his thighs and started to solidify. His attackers flew out of the trees, screaming in blood lust. Their fur was already covered in gore from previous kills.

Vek kept his eyes open, watching his death approaching. *Goodbye, Mia.*

A flash of movement to the right.

A woman leaped out of nowhere, swinging a wooden staff. She was lightning-quick. Her staff slammed into one alien, driving it to the ground. She swung the staff behind her, and sent another alien flying.

"Drak, woman, you can fight." Corsair appeared, firing a wicked-looking crossbow.

"Hit the plant with the flames," the woman yelled.

Corsair lit his next bolt on fire and sent it sailing into the heart of the gray plant. Flames ran up the spiky leaves and the plant shriveled in on itself, snuffing out the blaze.

Vek's vision blurred. His legs gave out from under

him, and he fell to his knees. He was so tired. He closed his eyes.

"Vek! Oh, God." Mia stepped in front of him, her horrified gaze on his legs. Her shaking hand cupped his cheek.

Galen, Raiden, and Thorin materialized. Galen hacked away the now-hard ooze trapping Vek. He felt more burning pain, and a second later, he was being lowered to the ground.

He looked up, blinking slowly, staring at the dome high overhead, and the clouds beyond it.

"The wounds are bad," Galen said. "The plant secretion has eaten his legs down to the bone beneath the knees."

"And he has skin burns from earlier plus a bad gut wound," Raiden added.

Mia leaned over Vek, tears sliding down her cheeks. One dripped onto his face. "You'll be okay. Hold on."

He stared into the face that meant so much to him. His Mia. His mate. "Everything I've suffered, I would suffer again for the chance to hold you in my arms."

"Vek." More tears poured down her cheeks.

"Mia, don't cry." He felt hands pressing against his legs, trying to staunch the flow of blood. Something was wrapped around them. "I die free and mated." He smiled at her.

"No." She cupped his cheeks, forcing his gaze to meet hers. "Don't leave me, Vek. I've searched my entire life for you. I traveled across the galaxy to find my place, and it's with you. All I've ever wanted is to find the thing that clicks, that feels right, that feeds my soul. All I've ever wanted is a person to love me just as I am. A person I love just as they are. Vek, you're my one thing. I love you."

Warmth filled him. He wanted to respond, but he couldn't get his lips to work anymore.

Then there was no pain. He blinked slowly, seeing Mia was sobbing, but no longer hearing any sound.

She leaned down and he felt the soft press of her lips against his.

But then the darkness swallowed him.

CHAPTER FOURTEEN

Mia had read stories about people's hearts breaking. She'd never really believed it.

Until now.

She felt such a terrible, wrenching pain in her chest, and she was sure her heart was tearing in two. There was so much blood, and Vek's legs were so badly damaged.

She looked up at Galen. "Save him."

Raiden was pressing wadded fabric against Vek's legs and wrapping them in his cloak. "The gut wound isn't as bad as it looks, but the bleeding from his legs won't stop. I've poured in all our med gel, but the wounds are too severe."

"Likely a toxin in the plant's secretion is designed to increase the bleeding," Thorin said.

"I fucking hate this place." Mia looked around wildly. Harper's face was filled with sadness, and Ryan had a hand pressed to her mouth, her eyes wide.

"He needs a regen tank," Galen said.

Mia tasted bile in her throat. She knew it was a long, arduous journey back to Kor Magna. He'd never make it. She swallowed, staring up at the dome, fighting back tears. On the inside, a scream wailed through her head.

Then she blinked. *Wait.* They were in the wreckage of a starship.

"Neve?" She glanced over at the woman. Neve was standing nearby, her staff held firmly in her hands, ready for an attack. "Have you seen any smaller ships in here? Shuttles? Escape pods?"

The woman frowned. "There's an area behind the dome where the Srinar do all their maintenance. It's full of engineering equipment. And that's where they breed new plants or heal any that have been damaged." She lifted a shoulder. "I've only been in there once, but I got caught quickly."

"We need to get back there," Mia said.

"The door is secure," Neve added. "I was able to slip in behind some Nerium guards the last time."

"I should be able to hack the door controls," Ryan said.

Galen lifted his chin. "Take us there. Thorin?" The big gladiator leaned down and lifted Vek.

They headed off, Neve leading the way.

"Why haven't you escaped?" Corsair asked Neve. "You seem to know the inside of this craft well, and the places where you can get out."

"None of your business." She pushed through a wall of green.

They had just cleared some thick vegetation, when two red-skinned fighters rushed at them. Raiden and

Harper leaped forward, moving in perfect unison. Raiden swung his sword, and Harper leaped high, twin swords in her hands. They brought the attackers down with a few hard, swift blows.

But as they moved again, several large, scale-covered animals skittered out from the trees, creeping closer on six legs. The gladiators and Corsair moved in. Neve leaped over the top of one creature, her deadly staff swinging in a blur. After a few tense moments, they had dispatched the beasts. A mere second later, the bushes ahead started shifting and moving, preparing to attack.

Mia's jaw clenched in frustration. The attacks were slowing them down so much, they were barely making any progress. She looked at Vek's still, drawn face. He didn't have much more time.

"The Srinar are watching all our moves," Galen said with a scowl.

"I can shut down the cameras." Ryan pushed her dark hair off her face. "Hell, maybe I can shut down the whole damn streaming system. But I have to plug in to do it."

"I'll show you where you can access it," Neve said. "But it's in the opposite direction of the maintenance bay."

"We'll split up," Galen ordered. He shot a look at Corsair.

The caravan master nodded. "I'll go with them."

Neve stiffened. "We don't need protection."

"I was hoping you'd protect me," Corsair said with a wink.

Neve's lips stayed flat, her face unamused.

"Go," Galen ordered. "We'll continue to the maintenance bay." He glanced at Ryan. "If we can't open the door, we'll be waiting for you to do it."

Ryan's nose wrinkled. "No pressure." Her gaze flicked to Vek. "I'll get you through."

Mia watched the small group disappear into the bushes and prayed they'd be okay.

"Stay close." Galen lifted his sword and took the lead.

They fought off two more sets of attackers, before they hacked through some thick bushes and found a small, open patch of grass. Mia's pulse leaped. On the other side of the patch stood a set of metal doors.

Galen stepped cautiously out into the clearing. Mia watched him assess their surroundings with a practiced eye, his posture indicating he was prepared for anything.

A buzzing sound filled the air, echoing off the trees.

"What now?" Raiden turned in a slow circle, scanning the vegetation.

Several large insects rose up out of some nearby bushes. Mia's chest hitched. They looked like enormous bees, with black-and-gray striped bodies, and large stingers behind them. *Great.* Mia liked bees, but she had a feeling these alien ones were going to ruin her appreciation.

Thorin growled, hitching Vek's body closer.

The bees' buzzing ramped up a notch, and then, without warning, the swarm attacked.

As the insects arrowed toward them, Galen, Raiden, and Harper charged forward, swinging their swords.

Thorin crouched, and Mia did the same, throwing herself over Vek's body. She heard Raiden let out a steady stream of curses, and she risked a glance. Bees were stinging the gladiators indiscriminately. The gladiators fought back, but the insects were quick, dodging the swords.

Mia felt an electric sting on her back and winced. Thorin waved a hand, knocking several bees away.

Anger charged through Mia. She felt another sting on her back, and the sticky wetness of Vek's blood soaking her front. Somewhere, on a distant planet, assholes were sitting in their comfy chairs, watching people *die* for fucking entertainment. She looked down into Vek's still face. Vek was suffering and dying, all for their sick pleasure.

Screw this. She jumped to her feet, snatched up a stick, and started batting the insects away.

But it was no good. They kept coming. She glanced around the open space. Raiden, Harper, and Galen's arms were covered in red welts from where they'd been stung.

Vek made a sound and Mia looked down. A bee was on his chest. She wrenched it off and threw it. Vek shifted sluggishly.

She stroked his face. "It's okay, babe. I'm here." Without thinking, she started to sing. It was a song she'd been working on since she'd arrived at the House of Galen. The lyrics flowed out of her. She closed her eyes and let her feelings flow into her voice.

It was a song about love, hope, and belonging. It was about trust and finding a person who'd never let you down. Who stood with you, without question.

About a man who saw deep inside her and made her

feel whole. Made her feel special.

Vek settled and turned his face into her palm. Mia stroked his beloved blue skin.

When the song ended and the last note died away, Mia heard silence. No buzzing, nothing. She turned and her eyes widened.

The bees were hovering, all focused on her.

As the silence grew, she heard some of them start buzzing again, their movements jerky and angry.

"Mia, keep singing," Galen said.

Mia swallowed and broke into *Amazing Grace.*

The alien bees quieted again, hovering as a group. As Mia kept singing, they started to sway.

She moved into *Hallelujah.*

Galen tore off his black cloak and tossed it over the bees. Mia kept singing, as the imperator carefully pinned the bees to the ground. Raiden and Harper brought some rocks over and secured the cloak on the grass.

"Well done," Harper said to Mia.

"I just sang."

"Well, it just saved our asses."

"And Vek seems calmer and more stable," Thorin added. Mia moved back to him, pressing her hand to his arm.

"Let's get through that door, and see if we can find medical supplies or a ship," Galen said.

They reached the classic, metal spaceship doors. Mia touched the control panel, but the lights just blinked merrily back at her. She tried several combinations, before she slammed her palm against it.

"Fuck." She felt like she was choking. They needed

to get through.

"We'll have to hope that Ryan can get it open." Galen turned, sword lifted, and watched the greenery around them.

"Come on, Ryan," Harper murmured.

Somewhere nearby, a creature's wild screech sounded.

Mia looked at Vek. His breathing was more labored, now. She stared at the wall of green.

Come on, Ryan. Please.

Ryan

RYAN TAPPED on the small screen, her fingers flying. She was flat on her belly in the grass, under some small trees. The control panel that Neve knew of was set into the ground, and had been hidden under a rock.

"Everything's turned around." Ryan muttered a curse, trying to work out this strange system. It was like nothing she'd seen before.

"Keep trying," Corsair said. He and Neve were standing above her, both of them continuously scanning their surroundings for any unwelcome guests. "Your friends' lives depend on it."

Ryan snorted. "Wow, thanks for the pep talk."

The man's brow creased. "Pep?"

Neve shook her head. "She means that you're an idiot."

Corsair stiffened. "I've punished people for far less

than that insult."

Neve lifted her chin, her hands tightening on her staff. "Try it, pirate."

"I am not a pirate. I'm a caravan master." Another wide, white smile. "You can call me master."

"In your dreams."

"Can you guys knock it off?" Ryan grumbled. She hit on something and the screen filled with symbols. "Yes! I got through the system to the Srinar part of it. They're piggybacking on the existing system in this old ship. The Srinar system, I'm familiar with." She tapped some more, and images appeared on the small screen.

Neve leaned over her shoulder. "Oh, good, you've got the camera feed up. We can see the others." Then her voice changed. "Uh, oh, they've got company."

Ryan's stomach did a slow turn. The others were being attacked by bees. Giant freaking bees.

"Get the Srinar cameras shut down, and that door open," Corsair said.

"I'm trying." Ryan's fingers flew over the screen. She shut out the sounds of the angry bees and the shouts of the gladiators.

Suddenly the sound of beautiful singing came through the screen. *What the hell?*

"Wow," Neve said. "Mia has a hell of a voice."

The trio watched on the screen as the bees calmed down, and Galen took care of them. *Amazing.* Corsair tapped Ryan's shoulder impatiently, and she got back to work. *Door controls. Camera controls.* Fucking Srinar and their stupid games. She was going to really mess things up for them.

Ryan fell completely into her zone. This was when everything inside her went still, when she was tapped in deep to a computer system, working her magic.

"Galen and the others are approaching the door," Corsair said.

"Almost there." Ryan kept tapping, moving through the system. *There!* "Got it! Doors are open. And—" she tapped one last time "—the cameras are off. The Srinar are blind."

"Nice work." Corsair's grin was blinding. The man had a rugged, handsome face that begged a woman to take a look—or ten. Ryan idly noted that Neve was studying him rather intently, as well.

"You still in their system?" he asked.

Ryan nodded.

"How about we mess up the Srinar's little operation a bit before we meet up with the others?"

Ryan nodded, determination filling her. "Excellent idea." She started deleting information. Anything and everything.

Some things were protected with really tough encryption, but she kept working, her fingers flying.

Then she stopped, scanning the data. Fighter records were flashing across the screen. What if there was information on Dayna in there, somewhere? Or other humans abducted by the Thraxians?

God, what she'd give for a portable data drive right now.

"Speed it up, Ryan." Corsair pulled a crossbow off his back, aiming it at the bushes ahead of them. "We have company."

Ryan didn't see anything, but she didn't doubt him. "I need a few more minutes."

Neve lifted her staff. "We can buy you some more time." She flashed Corsair a glance. "Or, at least, I know I can."

Corsair smiled again. This time, it was laced with challenge. "Try and keep up, Earth woman."

Ryan got back to work, conscious of Corsair and Neve moving away from her. Without a sound or a rustle, Nerium guards rushed out of the vegetation.

Yeah, the Srinar were probably going to throw everything they could at them to try and stop Ryan. *Delete. Delete. Delete.* She smiled grimly.

She saw Corsair explode into action, crossbow bolts firing in quick succession. He dived, rolled and kept firing. Neve was right beside him, jumping high and moving that wicked staff with deadly moves.

Holy hell, the two of them could fight. Ryan had always wanted to be badass, but she knew it required a whole lot of exercise, discipline, and probably early-morning training. Ryan did *not* do early mornings. She preferred to be a badass with her fingers and a computer screen.

The computer beneath her beeped, and suddenly information flooded the screen. So much data. They could use all of it to crush the Srinar and their operations. She needed to take this with her. Or maybe upload it, somewhere.

She quickly tapped in more commands, trying to make an outside connection. Maybe she could hack some random computer in Kor Magna, and hide the data there. She could recover it later.

"Pirate, throw me," Neve called out.

Ryan looked up again and saw Corsair grip Neve's waist. With a powerful flex of his muscled arms, he tossed her up into the air. As she flew, she spun, her staff taking down several guards. She landed in the center of several Nerium, in a crouch. Then she grinned and exploded upward, taking down more guards.

Suddenly, Ryan's screen blinked and changed. A sharp, masculine face appeared.

"There you are," the man drawled.

She tensed. If it wasn't the arrogant boy genius.

"Where have you been?" he asked.

Like she'd been sashaying around on a beachside vacation. "I don't have time for you, info-boy. This is life or death."

He frowned. "Can I help?"

She nodded. "I've hacked the Srinar system. I've accessed their data. All their data. I want everything here, to help shut them down and find others they've enslaved."

"All their data." A hungry look filled the man's fascinating, nebula-blue eyes. He cracked his knuckles and Ryan was caught for a second on how long and well-shaped his fingers were. "Let's do it, Ryan."

She got to work, and on the screen, she saw his face set with concentration as he buckled down on his end. She could see what he was doing, and dammit, it was ingenious. The man might be arrogant, but he was smart, as well.

Zhim's link connected, and Ryan quickly started uploading across it. "It's done. I have to go."

He stared directly at her. "I look forward to meeting you in person, Ryan Amaya Nagano of Earth. Don't get hurt coming home."

A strange feeling swirled in Ryan's belly. She gave the man a nod, and shut off the screen. She pushed to her feet, and saw that the ground was littered with green-skinned aliens.

Corsair and Neve were standing in the middle of it, back to back. The caravan master turned, sliding his crossbow onto his back with a smile. "I believe I took down one more than you."

Neve straightened. "You did not." She spun her staff up behind her back, glaring at him.

"I did," he insisted.

"You don't get credit for that last one. I'd already hit him twice. He was a soft target."

"A draw, then. We took down the same number."

"I hate cocky men." In a lightning-fast move, Neve dropped into a crouch and swept her leg out in a half circle. Her boot hit Corsair's legs, and knocked the man into a sprawl. His colorful curse filled the air.

Neve stood, pushing her dark curls back off her face. "Now, I officially took down one more than you."

Ryan tried to hide her smile as a disgruntled Corsair rose to his feet.

"Ah, sorry to interrupt the one-upmanship," Ryan said. "But I'm finished, and we need to get back to the others before they leave us here."

CHAPTER FIFTEEN

Mia slammed her hand against the door controls once more, useless anger churning inside her. She could hear the rattle of Vek's breath, and she wanted to scream.

All of a sudden, the door beeped and opened.

"Thank you, Ryan," she murmured. Beyond the door was like another world. The lush greenery and tangled vegetation gave way to metal walls and a floor in a dull, dark gray. Galen led them inside, the door sliding closed behind them.

Mia took in the rows of workbenches, tools, crates, and cages. Toward the back of the cavernous space, sat rows of hydroponic gardens, with plants floating in fluid underneath strings of bright lights.

Through another large doorway, she saw what she'd hoped to find.

Shuttles.

Mia broke into a jog. "Through here." There were

three ships, but two lay in pieces, with engine parts scattered beside them. It looked like someone was rebuilding them.

The third shuttle had a very different design. It was made of steel and a glass-like substance, in graceful, elegant lines. It had a small dome in the center, reminiscent of the large one in the wreck.

"I've never seen a ship like this," Galen said.

"It's in good condition." Mia ran her hand along the side of the hull. There were wear marks, but someone had cared for it. She studied the intact engines. "It is old, though."

"It looks like the same design as the larger ship," Harper noted.

Mia moved toward the shuttle door and frowned. There was no control panel that she could see, just the small, engraved image of some sort of flower on the side.

"It'll be risky to fly out over the desert," Galen said.

She met his gaze. "It's worth it. Besides, we'll head straight back to Kor Magna, and I don't care if this shuttle is falling apart by the time we get there, just as long as we get Vek back to the healers."

Galen nodded.

Suddenly, a banging echoed through the space. They all swiveled and looked back at the door they'd come through. Someone was trying to get in.

"Mia, can you fly it?" Galen asked.

Mia looked over to where Thorin was holding Vek's limp form. He was so still and covered in blood. The cloak hid his legs, but the image of how badly they were injured had already been burned into her brain.

"Yes," she said. "I can fly it."

Galen nodded. "Then let's get aboard."

Mia turned back to the ship. How the hell was she going to open it, let alone fly it? Every single insecurity she'd ever had poured over her in a rush. She wasn't smart enough, pretty enough, bold enough, or strong enough. But Vek, the man she was in love with, was depending on her.

She wouldn't fail him.

She pressed a hand to the metal of the door, trying to think where to start to open it. She felt a faint tingle under her palm and a vague sensation of being linked to the ship.

The door started to lower, and Mia leaped back. She pressed her palm to her thigh and fought back a wave of nausea. The sensation reminded her far too much about being plugged in to Catalyst's system. A ramp extended out of the shuttle.

"How did you do that?" Harper asked.

"No idea." Mia's heart knocked hard in her chest. "But let's go."

They all raced up the ramp and into the spacious shuttle. The main cabin contained several rows of elegantly shaped chairs, designed for beings even larger than Thorin. Everything was decorated in shades of cream and green. Mia continued to the cockpit, where two oversized pilots' chairs sat, facing a round bubble of glass.

"Lie him down here on the floor." Galen's voice. "Find some new bandages. We need to put more pressure on those wounds."

Mia blocked the bustle and conversation out, and leaned over the sleek, cream console. She touched the strange and foreign controls and buttons, but nothing she tried seemed to do anything.

"Mia." Harper leaned over her shoulder. "Look."

She peered through the glass at several Nerium and Srinar guards rushing in to the space. Laser fire hit the bubble, and made her flinch. Thankfully, the blasts reflected harmlessly off the ship.

"Can you retract the ramp?" Harper asked.

"No." She didn't even know how she had opened it.

Harper pulled her swords. "I'll make sure no one comes aboard."

Mia kept trying every combination of controls she could think of. Nothing was working. She slammed a fist against the console in frustration, tears blurring her eyes.

Dammit. Why couldn't she work this out?

She glanced behind her, and saw Vek flat on the floor, blood pooling beneath his body. And nothing in this damn shuttle was operational.

Suddenly, shouts sounded outside the shuttle. Through the glass, Mia watched a whirling blur come into view, followed by crossbow bolts slamming into the guards. She spotted Ryan's black hair flaring out behind her, as she ducked and weaved across the maintenance bay. Neve and Corsair followed closely.

"Harper!" Mia shouted. "The others are here."

"Roger that," Harper called back.

Seconds later, Ryan sprinted inside, Corsair right behind her.

"Where's Neve?" Galen asked.

"Right behind us." Corsair swiveled.

Mia shifted and saw Neve standing at the bottom of the ramp.

"Come on!" Corsair waved his hand.

Neve didn't head up the ramp. The woman lifted her hand, saluted, then spun and disappeared back into the maintenance bay. Mia saw her fighting her way back through the guards. *What the hell was she doing?*

Corsair cursed and took a step out on the ramp, but Galen gripped the man's shoulder. "There's no time."

"We can't leave her," Mia cried.

"We're losing him," Raiden called out.

Mia's heart lodged in her throat. *Vek*. She stared at the controls again. Neve had made her choice, and Mia would worry about her later. Right now, Vek needed help.

Mia blew out a breath and cleared her mind. She imagined she was back with Vek in that cave, his hard, warm body pressed to hers, his lips traveling over her skin. She let her hands move over the controls once more, trying to get something to work.

Ryan appeared beside her. "Let me see if I can help." She sat down in the copilot's chair beside Mia.

Together, the women quickly worked side-by-side.

"These are the basic controls," Ryan said, pointing at the console.

Mia swallowed. "The higher-level functions can only be accessed here." She pointed to a large spike on the console.

Ryan winced. "It looks like whoever designed the

ship physically spiked into the system to fly the ship. They must have had some way to physically link in."

Mia realized she was rubbing at the scar at her temple. Her own reminder of physically linking in. "Can we fly it without doing that?"

"I think so." Ryan's hands danced over the controls. "We have no idea what plugging directly into an unknown alien system could do to us."

The door closed and the ramp retracted. Damn, Ryan was a virtuoso, and a second later, the console flared to life, the shuttle vibrating as the engines engaged.

Ryan grinned at her. "Just don't ask me to fly the thing. That's all you."

"Deal." Mia quickly determined the ship's basic controls. *Hold on, Vek.* "Everyone hold on to something, or strap in. This might be a little bumpy." She clicked her own harness into place. It was far too big, but it was better than nothing.

As she pushed her palm against a control, the shuttle rose off the ground, the wings shaking, but thankfully not hitting anything. Mia stared straight ahead and focused on flying. She turned the shuttle to aim at the external doors at the end of the maintenance bay.

Ryan touched the co-pilot controls. "Give me a sec. *There.*" The doors started to retract.

Mia sent the ship forward. Too fast. The left wing scraped against the wall, jerking the shuttle. She heard someone stumble and grunt. "Sorry," she called, distractedly.

But a moment later, they shot out of the doors and

were soaring out over the mountains. The beige sands of the desert lay ahead of them.

"Woo-hoo, Mia." Ryan leaned over and clapped her on the shoulder. "Nice work!"

"Thanks for the help." Mia stared straight ahead, her muscles locked tight as she concentrated on flying the ship. "Now, let me fly this thing." She only had the most basic of controls, but it would have to do.

She didn't look back at Vek, but in her head, she could picture his pale face, his blood-smeared skin and the terrible wounds. She *would* get him back to the House of Galen.

She urged more speed from the ship. They hit turbulence, the ship vibrating. The left wing tipped down and Mia overcorrected and the right wing tipped down. They wobbled from side to side, gladiators grumbling, before she smoothed them out the best she could. She couldn't risk going any faster, or she might lose control of the entire ship.

The minutes ticked by, and she kept her hands tight on the controls.

"His vitals are destabilizing," Harper yelled. "More pressure, Raiden."

"His heart's giving up," Galen said.

Mia's heart lodged in her throat. "Keep an eye on the controls." She unclipped and leaped out of her chair.

"What?" Ryan squeaked. "Mia, no—"

"I'll be back." She raced to Vek's side. The others parted and let her close.

God, his skin was so pale. She rubbed her thumb over

his lips and cupped his jaw. "I'm here, Vek. I need you to stay with me. Hold on a little longer." *Please.*

She pressed her hand to his chest. His normally strong heartbeat was just a flutter. Tears burned her eyes.

"I can't lose you, babe." She started humming an old Scottish folk song, before softly crooning the lyrics. It recalled the escape of a prince after his loss in a battle. The shuttle fell silent as she sang.

"His heartbeat is steadier," Galen said. "Keep singing, Mia."

She moved into another song, one of her own. She'd written it a few weeks ago, about taking a long journey, holding the hands of friends. Of carrying on, even when she was weary. Of filling the day with joy and happiness, to carry her through the darkness. Of opening her heart, and letting love free.

Mia let the last note linger, then pressed a kiss to Vek's lips.

"You have an amazing gift," Thorin murmured.

"His pulse is steadier and his color is better," Harper said.

An alarm sounded, filling the cockpit.

"Oh, God," Ryan cried. "Mia, I need you up here!"

Mia hurried back to the pilot's chair. Kor Magna lay on the horizon like a glittering jewel. The distinctive walls of the arena were just visible.

"What's wrong?"

"We're losing altitude." Ryan's dark eyes were wide. "Nothing I've done is bringing us back up."

Mia's gut clenched. She touched the controls but saw they'd lost some of the systems. The engines weren't responding and they were slowly gliding downward. She suspected the desert was wreaking havoc on the old ship and her engines.

The pilot in her did the mental calculations. They'd crash into the sand before they reached the city.

Then she heard Raiden's urgent tone. "His heart just stopped."

No! Mia swiveled to look back.

Ryan urged her forward. "Just focus on flying, Mia. That's the best way to help him now."

Mia's jaw locked and she nodded, fighting back the tears blurring her eyes.

"Out of my way." Harper's voice. "I need to do CPR."

Mia closed her eyes for a second. *No.* She had to save Vek. She opened her eyes and stared at the spike on the console. Her throat tightened. Vek was everything to her, and so were her new friends. He'd waded back into his worst fear to save her and she sure as hell would do the same for him.

She sucked in a breath and slammed her hand down on the spike.

"Mia!" Ryan cried.

The pain was sharp, but then faded as information poured into Mia's head. Again, she felt that connection to the ship. It was stronger than before and in her head, she imagined the shuttle rising up.

The ship obeyed. She searched out where the engines were damaged and set the system to work on containing the problem.

"What the—?" Ryan stared at her.

Mia felt a sense of calm wash over her. She was getting Vek to Medical, whatever it took. Mentally, she turned the shuttle, aiming for the heart of the city.

"We got him back," Harper called out.

Mia felt a spurt of relief. "Where should I land?"

"The arena." Galen appeared at her shoulder.

Mia nodded. She adjusted course and they cruised in. Then she felt a sharp pain in her head. She winced, just as the ship listed to one side.

"We just lost an engine," Ryan said, her head craned to look out the window.

Another pain and Mia felt the second engine faltering. "I'm losing the final engine." She could see the flames in her head. "Trying to fix the damage." But she felt her control of the ship slipping away. "I'm losing control!"

The ship started to shudder.

A muscle ticked in Galen's jaw. "Mia, I need you to patch through a comm call for me."

A wave of nausea washed through Mia and she swallowed it back. God, they were going to crash into the homes of poor, innocent people. "Where to?"

"The Dark Nebula Casino."

Mia nodded and mentally placed the call. After a minute that felt like an hour, a woman's face appeared on the console screen. She was stunning, with perfect features, and pink-and-blonde hair swept up in an elegant twist. She had a smiling, pleasant look on her face.

"Welcome to the Dark Nebula Casino." Her voice was a modulated purr.

Galen leaned forward. "Rillian. Now."

The woman's smile dissolved. "Yes, Imperator. One moment, please."

The screen went blank, displaying a glowing, silver spiral that Mia assumed was the logo of the Dark Nebula. A wave of pain hit at the base of her skull. She gritted her teeth, fighting to keep some control of the alien ship.

The next thing, a man's face appeared on the screen.

"Holy cow," Ryan muttered. "Bare chests and muscles were bad enough, now they are making them so handsome you want to weep in gratitude."

Mia knew the dark-haired man was Rillian. A wealthy casino owner, and ally of the House of Galen.

"Galen." A deep drawl.

"Rillian. We need your help."

Rillian tilted his head. "Go on."

"We are coming in over Kor Magna in an ancient shuttle that we're losing control of. Vek's been badly injured. We need to land in the arena without killing ourselves or anyone else."

The casino owner blinked his midnight-dark eyes. "Well, the House of Galen doesn't do dull, does it?" He turned and barked some orders at people out of view. "Hold tight and let me see what I can do."

"Thank you," Mia said.

Rillian glanced at her and nodded.

"I'll owe you," Galen said.

"There are no debts between friends." The screen went blank.

Mia's hand tightened on the armrest of her chair. She was doing everything she could to maintain her connection to the ship, but now pain was exploding through her head. They were flying over the city now, the skyscrapers of the District ahead, and she swallowed. She wanted to help Vek, but she didn't want to crash land and hurt people, either. She counted each heartbeat as it reverberated in her ears. She kept coaxing the failing engine to keep them in the air.

She was excruciatingly conscious of Harper breathing and pumping Vek's chest behind her to keep him alive.

All of a sudden, there was a *whoosh* of sound and two other ships passed overhead. Mia gasped. They looked like spiders flying in the air. They had solid gray bodies, and six "legs", that were actually articulated crane arms.

"Galen ship, this is Dark Nebula One." A voice came through the comm unit. "Prepare for attachment. We'll help you down."

Relief burst in Mia's chest. "Acknowledged, Dark Nebula One. Tell me what you need."

The Dark Nebula pilot talked her through the landing sequence. The two cargo ships locked onto the alien shuttle, making it jolt in midair.

"You'll need to keep the ship level and the speed steady," the pilot said.

"I'll do what I can."

"You don't and you'll crash."

"I'll do it," she said. *For Vek.*

They started their descent.

Mia ground her teeth together, sweat breaking out on her brow. The ship was fighting her.

"Galen, she's killing herself," Ryan said.

"She can do it." Galen's tone was filled with assurance. "I know it."

Hell, yes, she'd do it. She felt a trickle of fluid out of her nose and tasted blood in her mouth. She'd bitten her tongue.

"God, we're losing him again," Harper shouted.

Hold on, Vek. Almost there. Mia thought of all the lyrics she'd scribbled in her journals. She started to sing.

About love.

About finding your one.

About Vek.

A hush filled the shuttle and she heard murmurs from the Dark Nebula pilots. As she sang, she poured everything she had into the song and felt the ship stop shuddering.

The oval of sand on the arena floor grew larger and larger. They hit the ground with a hard bump, and Mia was tossed forward, her straps digging into her shoulders. A spray of sand hit the windshield.

But they were down.

"Thank you, Dark Nebula." Adrenaline charged through Mia. *They were down.* She tore her hand off the spike. Ryan was there a second later, pressing wadded fabric to the wound.

"Our pleasure," the pilot answered. "Just hearing you sing is payment enough. I've never heard anything as beautiful and touching." The pilot cleared his throat, sounding embarrassed. "Decoupling now."

Another jolt, but Mia was already ripping her harness off and bounding to her feet.

"Get him to Medical," Galen ordered.

She saw that Thorin had ripped one of the seats out. He and Raiden were holding it like a stretcher. Vek was laid out on it, Harper straddling him, pumping his chest.

They moved down the still-descending ramp, and Mia sprinted out after them.

A crowd had gathered, staring at the ship in the middle of the arena with wide eyes. But Mia didn't pay them any attention. Soon, the gladiators raced into the tunnels, heading for the House of Galen.

Mia was numb as they entered the House and then Medical. Everything around her became a flurry of activity, and she felt removed from it, like she was floating above, disconnected. Even the usually unflappable Hermia healers looked worried, as they started treating Vek.

She tried to get closer, but Raiden pulled her back.

"Let them work," he said.

Mia could see the full extent of his injuries and tears flowed down her cheeks. The bottom half of his legs were...gone. She tasted bile in her mouth, and fought it down. It was bad. She was well aware that he might still die or lose his legs. All because of her. She saw Winter push in close to Vek, her brow creased.

Before Mia knew it, they were putting Vek into one of the regen tanks at the back of the room.

"All we can do now is hope that we caught his injuries in time," one of the tall, slender, and genderless healers said in a calm voice. "He is strong, and in good physical condition. If his injuries can be healed, the regen tank will do it."

Harper slid an arm around Mia. "Come and get some rest."

She shook her head. "I'm not leaving him."

Winter appeared, holding some med gel. "Let me see to your hand."

Mia kept her gaze on the tank and let Winter treat her hand.

Harper hugged her. "I'll check back on you later. Do you need anything?"

Emotions churned inside Mia, strong and overwhelming. She needed to write and get them out. "There's a notebook in my room. Where I write down my lyrics."

"I'll bring it."

After everyone had gone, Mia sank down on the ground beside the regen tank, and pressed her face and hands to the clear side. She stared at Vek's body, hanging there in the blue gel.

"Be okay, Vek. I haven't told you how much I love you, yet." Mia closed her eyes, fighting her sobs back. "Don't leave me."

MIA FELT strong arms lifting her. The blankets and pillow someone had given her slipped away. She fought back the fog of exhaustion and lifted her head.

Vek's face filled her vision.

She stiffened. "Vek."

"Shh." Golden eyes were pinned on her as he carried her out of Medical.

"You're okay?" She tried to see his legs. Two long days had passed since he'd been placed in the regen tank. Two excruciating days that he'd been unconscious, the tank slowly regenerating his legs. Winter had spent time talking to her about the incredible gel in the tank and its mix of sugar molecules and proteins that could replace damaged tissue and rebuild muscle. Two days of torment as Mia had prayed for him to open his eyes.

"I said quiet, Mia. I am fine, but you have not been taking care of yourself." His tone warned her he wasn't happy.

But Mia was ecstatic. Vek was *alive*. She stayed quiet, leaning into him and absorbing the heat of his body. When he carried her up some stairs, she realized that he was taking her up to the rooftop garden.

He strode through the greenery, and sat her down on the same pillows where they'd first touched each other. She saw that a tray of food had been set out and beside it was her lyrics journal. How had that gotten here?

Vek shifted and her focus shifted back to him. "You're really okay?" She reached out and stroked his hard thigh. His trousers were filled out perfectly.

"Yes." He picked up some succulent fruit and pressed it to her mouth. "I was unhappy to hear that you were not taking care of yourself while I was healing. You spent hours by the regen tank."

She chewed the sweet, tart fruit. "I couldn't rest until I knew you were okay. And I spent a lot of that time writing."

He fed her another piece of fruit. "I know. I had Harper read me your songs."

Mia felt a flush of...something. Nerves, embarrassment, fear. "What...what did you think?"

"They are beautiful, Mia. Even more beautiful when you sing them." He cupped her cheeks. "I could feel your love in every word."

"I love you, Vek." It felt so good to tell him.

He growled. "I love you, too, Mia. Completely." It glowed in his eyes as his head lowered.

His kiss was firm, deep, and Mia threw herself into it. When she pulled back, she saw his gaze was hot now. Her gaze dropped down, and she stared at the erection straining his pants.

"I think you really are feeling better."

"Mia." A deep rumble. His arms wrapped around her, pulling her close. His mouth pressed against hers.

"I thought I was going to lose you." Her voice cracked.

"Galen told me you flew an alien ship and got me back here. That you were forced to link with the system, which I know you hate after Catalyst's violation—"

"I'd do it again in a heartbeat."

"You saved my life...again."

She teased his lips with hers. "I guess we're even, then."

Vek sat back against the cushions, turning her and pulling her between his legs. She snuggled her back into him. Then he took his time, picking the choicest bits of food from the platter and feeding them to her. In between her bites, his big hands stroked down her arms, across her collarbones.

"Landing a ship in the middle of the arena was kind

of a big deal," she said. "Galen sent a team in to dismantle it and take it to some warehouse that Rillian, an ally of the House of Galen, owns. Apparently, they think the ship belongs to *the* Creators. The advanced aliens who created life throughout the galaxy."

"I don't care about the ship, Mia. I only care about you. I would like to care for you forever."

Her breath caught, and she craned her neck to look back. "Vek—"

"I have little to offer you. I have no job, no purpose—"

She twisted on her knees to face him. "I only want you, and that's not a little, that's everything. I love you, Vek."

He made a low, growling sound, and pressed his face to her hair. "Will you be my mate, Mia?"

Her chest filled to bursting, that familiar sense of rightness falling over her. "It would be my honor."

He kissed her again—deep and long. "I don't remember my world, my people, or my family. But I do recall a tradition to seal a mating."

Mia saw the heat in his gaze. "Oh?"

"A male must hunt his female down and capture her. If she agrees to his claim, they are mated."

"Hunt her down?"

Vek lifted her to her feet. "Go."

Mia looked down at him, her heart beating hard. "What?"

"Run, Mia. Evade, hide, run—" his voice lowered "—but know that when I find you, I will claim you and fuck you hard."

Excitement flared inside her. "Vek—"

"Run," he growled.

Mia squealed, spun, and sprinted into the trees. Her breathing was fast, her pulse jumping wildly. She pushed through some bushes.

Behind her, she heard a growl.

She swallowed a cry, and ducked through a row of fruit trees, then around a pair of garden beds. The sweet smell of some flowers hit her nose, and she pushed through a wall of vines.

There was none of the dread of the Srinar hunting grounds here. In this place, the vegetation was all for pleasure.

Mia paused, crouching down and listening. All she could hear was her heartbeat pounding in her ears.

This was fun, exciting. The sexiest kind of play. Everything that she and Vek hadn't had for so long.

She heard a rustle nearby, and with her blood pumping, she turned and ran.

But she'd only taken two steps when arms grabbed her from behind. They wrapped around her and lifted her off her feet. She squealed.

His hot mouth was on her neck and she felt the scrape of his teeth. She arched into him.

Vek carried her back to the cushions, and then she was being pushed down onto the soft coverings. She watched as he tore her clothes off.

He shoved her legs apart, his big hard body covering hers. "Mia, do you accept my claim?"

"Yes, yes."

The head of his cock prodded between her legs, and

with need driving her, she tilted her hips up. He thrust inside her.

Mia arched her back, a cry ripping from her throat.

"I love you, Mia. Now and always. I will protect you, fight for you, be yours always."

"Vek." He was thrusting into her with wild, primal abandon. "I love you, too. Don't stop."

It didn't take long for them to find release. Vek's deep groan mixed with her cries.

Mia had found the exact place where she belonged. In the arms of her blue-skinned alien.

CHAPTER SIXTEEN

Vek walked down the corridor beside Mia, and realized he felt happy and calm.

Everything was right in his world.

He gripped Mia's slender fingers more tightly. He was in love with his mate, and she loved him. Just a few short months ago, he'd never, ever imagined he'd have Mia in his life.

He could hardly believe that he'd gone from prisoner, slave, and killer, to a free man and the mate of a beautiful woman who had agreed to be his.

"Come on." Mia led him toward a doorway. "I'm eager to see if they found anything about Dayna in the records Ryan stole from the Srinar."

They were deep in the bowels of the House of Galen, having just passed some maintenance workers fixing pieces of equipment. They continued through a doorway, and ahead, he saw Ryan sitting behind a bank of computers, with Rory at her shoulder. The two were muttering about things Vek had no clue about.

Ryan looked better. She looked rested, and well-fed, her dark, shiny hair brushing her shoulders.

Suddenly Rory looked at the screen and let out a loud laugh. "Oh, Zhim will *hate* that."

"What?" Mia asked.

The women looked up at them. Ryan smiled, and Rory looked at their joined hands and winked.

Rory rubbed her big belly. "Ryan just hung up on Zhim. He was being an ass and deserved it. He decoded some of the information that Ryan sent him from the Srinar hunting grounds, but—"

"Decided he wasn't going to share it," Ryan said, incensed.

"So while Ryan was verbally ripping him a new one, she snuck into his system, copied the data, and then deleted it off his system." Rory threw her head back and laughed again. "Then she hung up on him."

Vek didn't know Zhim all that well, but he knew that the information merchant would not like having someone break into his system, or having information taken away.

Ryan gave them a satisfied smile. "Oh, knowing him, I'm sure he will have made multiple backup copies."

Rory patted her belly. "It's still priceless."

Ryan grinned smugly. "True."

"Ryan, how are you?" Mia asked.

The woman tilted her head, a hint of resignation in her expression. "I'm free, so I'm good. I know we can't go back to Earth, but I'm planning to send a message home to let them know I'm okay, even if I have to work with Zhim to do it."

"You have family?" Vek asked.

Ryan nodded. "My parents, and one overprotective brother. David's probably lost his mind since I went missing." She cleared her throat. "And I have a fiancé. Sort-of."

"Sort of?" Rory's eyebrows rose. "I'm pretty sure being engaged is like being pregnant. You either are, or you aren't."

A flush of pink filled Ryan's cheeks. "Charlie and I have known each other a long time. It was sort of more assumed than official..."

Rory snorted.

"Leave her alone," Mia said. "Is your room okay?"

"It's a great room," Ryan said. "A huge bed, loads of clothes. After months of wearing the same freaking outfit, it is nice to have choices. And scary Galen and Rory set me up with this." She waved at the comp system.

"Galen's got an ulterior motive," Rory said. "If you can do the work he needs done, he won't have to hire Zhim, who costs a ton of money." Rory reached for a bowl resting beside the comp screen and fished out a handful of some sort of nuts. She started popping them into her mouth.

"Did I hear my name?" Galen entered the room, a tight, black shirt covering his chest and his black cloak falling behind him. Kace was with him, and the tall gladiator moved instantly to his woman, pulling Rory in for a kiss. His big hands covered her belly protectively.

Vek studied the couple. Kace did not show much

emotion, while Rory let everything show on her face. But now that Vek had Mia, he could recognize the looks on their faces. Love.

He suspected it was exactly the same look he wore when he looked at Mia. He pulled her in close to his side.

"You've recovered?" Galen asked Vek.

He nodded. "Thank you. For everything you have done."

Galen inclined his head.

Mia smiled. "By the way, Vek and I have made it official." She beamed at them all. "We're mated."

"Congratulations!" Rory hurried over to hug Mia, and then threw her arms around Vek.

He stilled, the hard mound of her belly a curious pressure against him. Then he felt a definite kick and he jerked.

"Sorry." Rory stepped back, rubbing her belly. "This mini gladiator has a kick like an enraged mule trying out for the NFL."

Vek had no idea what a mule or the NFL was. However, he saw Kace was smiling with pride, so he figured it was a good thing.

But then Mia's gaze moved back to Ryan and her smile dissolved. "Any luck locating Dayna? Or tracking Neve?"

Ryan's face fell. "Nothing, I'm sorry. I'm still combing through all the Srinar data. There has to be something in there about Dayna." Ryan's tone hardened. "But I won't stop looking. We won't abandon her."

"And Neve?" Mia asked.

Ryan shook her head. "The woman is a ghost."

When Mia leaned into him, Vek sensed her sadness. Instantly, he wanted to ease it. He spun her into his arms. "I promised you that we'd find them. We won't give up."

Mia nodded, pressing her cheek to his chest. "It just feels so wrong to be so happy when I know they're out there, somewhere, all alone."

"We will continue, no matter what," Vek murmured. "As will they."

"Vek," Galen said.

Vek lifted his head and looked at the imperator.

"The healers tell me that the drug cravings and aggressive bursts in your system have eased. They believe that the mating frenzy caused some biological response that helped cleanse your body."

Mia made a small sound and the faintest flush crept into her cheeks.

"You're more likely still prone to aggression, but you'll be able to control your responses and channel them. When you are ready, I'd like to invite you to train with my gladiators. You're House of Galen, now."

Vek went still, and sensed Mia holding her breath. Something in his chest tightened. He'd never belonged anywhere before.

He turned the offer over in his head. He'd been wondering what he was going to do with himself. This was a chance for him to contribute to the House of Galen, and to make something of himself. To use the skills that he'd so abhorred for something else...and to never have to fight to the death again.

He nodded at Galen. "It will be my honor to wear the House of Galen colors."

Mia's hands tightened on him, her face glowing with happiness.

Galen reached out an arm, and Vek pressed his forearm to the other man's. A warrior's clasp.

Then the imperator looked at Mia. "I've also been fielding several calls from Rillian for you, Mia."

Vek growled and she shot him an exasperated look before looking back at Galen. "What does Rillian want with me?"

"He heard you sing on the shuttle, and he discovered that you write your own songs. He'd like to talk to you about performing at the Dark Nebula Casino." Galen's lips quirked. "I believe he mentioned something about me being a greedy imperator for keeping such an incredible gift within the House of Galen and not sharing it. And also something about paying you a small fortune for your talents."

Mia's mouth dropped open. "He wants me to perform? And pay me for it?"

"Pay you an obscene amount of money for it."

She blinked and Vek sensed her stunned disbelief. He looked at her with pride, their gazes meeting. Mia had such talent and he knew it would be wrong to hold her back from sharing it.

She swallowed. "Um, tell Rillian I'll think about it."

"One more thing, Vek," Ryan said, standing. "I found your species listed in the Srinar database."

Mia gasped and Vek felt his stomach jump.

"The Nerium were the ones to take you from your homeworld."

That meant the vague fragments of memories of

being snatched by Nerium were real. Now his heart started beating hard against his ribs. Mia reached out and grabbed his hand.

"You're a Solokhian," Ryan said.

The name settled inside him. He didn't recognize it, consciously, but it felt right.

"I'm sorry, but the exact location of your planet isn't listed in the data, but it does seem that it's a long way from here," Ryan added. "It is listed as orbiting a large, very bright blue star and was dominated by blue vegetation. Makes sense. If the sun is brighter and blue, the vegetation would have a blue tint to reflect the light."

"I knew it," Mia murmured.

"There is a record of the Nerium stealing several children from Solokh. They were viciously pursued by Solokhian ships, and barely made it out alive. The Solokhian ships were not designed for long-range space travel and the Nerium never went back."

A tumble of different feelings washed through Vek. He hadn't been abandoned or thrown out like trash.

"Vek?" Mia's quiet voice.

He looked down at her. It was nice to have answers to questions that he'd always wondered about, but it didn't change things. His past was his past, and Mia was his life now.

"I'm okay," he said. "It is good that I have a name to give to our children."

Mia smiled.

"Speaking of children," Ryan continued. "I see some notes in here on the Solokhian species. They mate for life, and have a chemical reaction in their bodies that binds them to their mate."

Chemical reaction or not, Mia was his, and Vek would never let her go.

"And, uh, they give birth to three or four babies at once," Ryan said.

Mia straightened like she'd been struck. "What?"

"A litter." Rory elbowed Kace. "Glad your super sperm only made one alien bub."

Vek pulled Mia closer. "Mia is far too small to be pregnant with three or four younglings at once."

"One day we're going to have babies." Mia's face turned dreamy. "They'll be gorgeous, with blue skin and golden eyes—"

"No." He wouldn't risk his Mia. "No babies."

Her eyes narrowed. "Yes."

"No."

Mia crossed her arms. "We'll discuss this later."

"My money's on Mia," Rory whispered, but Vek had no trouble hearing it.

Galen cleared his throat. "One thing I've learned is that Earth women somehow seem to always get their own way."

Vek felt a spurt of fear, but then Mia reached up and cupped his cheeks. She pulled him down for a kiss. She laughed against his lips and everything else fell away.

"You and me, babe," she murmured. "We'll make it all work. Together."

Right here in his arms was his everything. The past that had scarred him for so long, was now just something that had led him to Mia.

And the future was laid out ahead of them, filled with freedom and bright shining opportunities. But most of all, it would be filled with love.

I hope you enjoyed Vek and Mia's story!

Galactic Gladiators continues with ROGUE which contains two novellas. The first stars information merchant Zhim who finds himself confounded by human hacker Ryan. The second stars caravan master Corsair who collides with the mysterious and prickly Neve. Coming November 2017.

For more action-packed romance, read on for a preview of the first chapter of *Marcus,* the first book in my best-selling Hell Squad series.

Don't miss out! For updates about new releases, action romance info, free books, and other fun stuff, sign up for my VIP mailing list and get your *free box set* containing three action-packed romances.

Click here to get started: www.annahackettbooks.com

FREE BOX SET DOWNLOAD

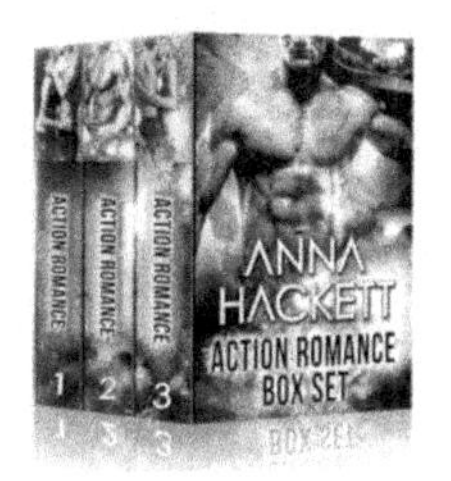

JOIN THE ACTION-PACKED ADVENTURE!

PREVIEW - HELL SQUAD: MARCUS

READY FOR ANOTHER?

IN THE AFTERMATH OF AN ALIEN INVASION:

HEROES WILL RISE... WHEN THEY HAVE SOMEONE TO LIVE FOR

Her team was under attack.

Elle Milton pressed her fingers to her small earpiece. "Squad Six, you have seven more raptors inbound from the east." Her other hand gripped the edge of her comp screen, showing the enhanced drone feed.

She watched, her belly tight, as seven glowing red dots converged on the blue ones huddled together in the burned-out ruin of an office building in downtown

Sydney. Each blue dot was a squad member and one of them was their leader.

"Marcus? Do you copy?" Elle fought to keep her voice calm. No way she'd let them hear her alarm.

"Roger that, Elle." Marcus' gravelly voice filled her ear. Along with the roar of laser fire. "We see them."

She sagged back in her chair. This was the worst part. Just sitting there knowing that Marcus and the others were fighting for their lives. In the six months she'd been comms officer for the squad, she'd worked hard to learn the ropes. But there were days she wished she was out there, aiming a gun and taking out as many alien raptors as she could.

You're not a soldier, Ellianna. No, she was a useless party-girl-turned-survivor. She watched as a red dot disappeared off the screen, then another, and another. She finally drew a breath. Marcus and his team were the experienced soldiers. She'd just be a big fat liability in the field.

But she was a damn good comms officer.

Just then, a new cluster of red dots appeared near the team. She tapped the screen, took a measurement. "Marcus! More raptors are en route. They're about one kilometer away. North." God, would these invading aliens ever leave them alone?

"Shit," Marcus bit out. Then he went silent.

She didn't know if he was thinking or fighting. She pictured his rugged, scarred face creased in thought as he formulated a plan.

Then his deep, rasping voice was back. "Elle, we need an escape route and an evac now. Shaw's been hit in the leg, Cruz is carrying him. We can't engage more raptors."

She tapped the screen rapidly, pulling up drone images and archived maps. *Escape route, escape route.* Her mind clicked through the options. She knew Shaw was taller and heavier than Cruz, but the armor they wore had slim-line exoskeletons built into them allowing the soldiers to lift heavier loads and run faster and longer than normal. She tapped the screen again. *Come on.* She needed somewhere safe for a Hawk quadcopter to set down and pick them up.

"Elle? We need it now!"

Just then her comp beeped. She looked at the image and saw a hazy patch of red appear in the broken shell of a nearby building. The heat sensor had detected something else down there. Something big.

Right next to the team.

She touched her ear. "Rex! Marcus, a rex has just woken up in the building beside you."

"Fuck! Get us out of here. Now."

Oh, God. Elle swallowed back bile. Images of rexes, with their huge, dinosaur-like bodies and mouths full of teeth, flashed in her head.

More laser fire ripped through her earpiece and she heard the wild roar of the awakening beast.

Block it out. She focused on the screen. Marcus needed her. The team needed her.

"Run past the rex." One hand curled into a tight fist, her nails cutting into her skin. "Go through its hiding place."

"Through its nest?" Marcus' voice was incredulous. "You know how territorial they are."

"It's the best way out. On the other side you'll find a railway tunnel. Head south along it about eight hundred meters, and you'll find an emergency exit ladder that you can take to the surface. I'll have a Hawk pick you up there."

A harsh expulsion of breath. "Okay, Elle. You've gotten us out of too many tight spots for me to doubt you now."

His words had heat creeping into her cheeks. His praise...it left her giddy. In her life BAI—before alien invasion—no one had valued her opinions. Her father, her mother, even her almost-fiancé, they'd all thought her nothing more than a pretty ornament. Hell, she *had* been a silly, pretty party girl.

And because she'd been inept, her parents were dead. Elle swallowed. A year had passed since that horrible night during the first wave of the alien attack, when their giant ships had appeared in the skies. Her parents had died that night, along with most of the world.

"Hell Squad, ready to go to hell?" Marcus called out.

"Hell, yeah!" the team responded. "The devil needs an ass-kicking!"

"Woo-hoo!" Another voice blasted through her headset, pulling her from the past. "Ellie, baby, this dirty alien's nest stinks like Cruz's socks. You should be here."

A smile tugged at Elle's lips. Shaw Baird always knew how to ease the tension of a life-or-death situation.

"Oh, yeah, Hell Squad gets the best missions," Shaw added.

Elle watched the screen, her smile slipping. Everyone called Squad Six the Hell Squad. She was never quite sure if it was because they were hellions, or because they got sent into hell to do the toughest, dirtiest missions.

There was no doubt they were a bunch of rebels. Marcus had a rep for not following orders. Just the previous week, he'd led the squad in to destroy a raptor outpost but had detoured to rescue survivors huddled in an abandoned hospital that was under attack. At the debrief, the general's yelling had echoed through the entire base. Marcus, as always, had been silent.

"Shut up, Shaw, you moron." The deep female voice carried an edge.

Elle had decided there were two words that best described the only female soldier on Hell Squad—loner and tough. Claudia Frost was everything Elle wasn't. Elle cleared her throat. "Just get yourselves back to base."

As she listened to the team fight their way through the rex nest, she tapped in the command for one of the Hawk quadcopters to pick them up.

The line crackled. "Okay, Elle, we're through. Heading to the evac point."

Marcus' deep voice flowed over her and the tense muscles in her shoulders relaxed a fraction. They'd be back soon. They were okay. He was okay.

She pressed a finger to the blue dot leading the team. "The bird's en route, Marcus."

"Thanks. See you soon."

She watched on the screen as the large, black shadow of the Hawk hovered above the ground and the team boarded. The rex was headed in their direction, but they were already in the air.

Elle stood and ran her hands down her trousers. She shot a wry smile at the camouflage fabric. It felt like a dream to think that she'd ever owned a very expensive, designer wardrobe. And heels—God, how long had it been since she'd worn heels? These days, fatigues were all that hung in her closet. Well-worn ones, at that.

As she headed through the tunnels of the underground base toward the landing pads, she forced herself not to run. She'd see him—them—soon enough. She rounded a corner and almost collided with someone.

"General. Sorry, I wasn't watching where I was going."

"No problem, Elle." General Adam Holmes had a military-straight bearing he'd developed in the United Coalition Army and a head of dark hair with a brush of distinguished gray at his temples. He was classically handsome, and his eyes were a piercing blue. He was the top man in this last little outpost of humanity. "Squad Six on their way back?"

"Yes, sir." They fell into step.

"And they secured the map?"

God, Elle had almost forgotten about the map. "Ah, yes. They got images of it just before they came under attack by raptors."

"Well, let's go welcome them home. That map might just be the key to the fate of mankind."

They stepped into the landing areas. Staff in various military uniforms and civilian clothes raced around. After the raptors had attacked, bringing all manner of vicious creatures with them to take over the Earth, what was left of mankind had banded together.

Whoever had survived now lived here in an underground base in the Blue Mountains, just west of Sydney, or in the other, similar outposts scattered across the planet. All arms of the United Coalition's military had been decimated. In the early days, many of the surviving soldiers had fought amongst themselves, trying to work out who outranked whom. But it didn't take long before General Holmes had unified everyone against the aliens. Most squads were a mix of ranks and experience, but the teams eventually worked themselves out. Most didn't even bother with titles and rank anymore.

Sirens blared, followed by the clang of metal. Huge doors overhead retracted into the roof.

A Hawk filled the opening, with its sleek gray body and four spinning rotors. It was near-silent, running on a small thermonuclear engine. It turned slowly as it descended to the landing pad.

Her team was home.

She threaded her hands together, her heart beating a little faster.

Marcus was home.

Marcus Steele wanted a shower and a beer.

Hot, sweaty and covered in raptor blood, he leaped down from the Hawk and waved at his team to follow. He kept a sharp eye on the medical team who raced out to tend to Shaw. Dr. Emerson Green was leading them, her white lab coat snapping around her curvy body. The blonde doctor caught his gaze and tossed him a salute.

Shaw was cursing and waving them off, but one look from Marcus and the lanky Australian sniper shut his mouth.

Marcus swung his laser carbine over his shoulder and scraped a hand down his face. Man, he'd kill for a hot shower. Of course, he'd have to settle for a cold one since they only allowed hot water for two hours in the morning in order to conserve energy. But maybe after that beer he'd feel human again.

"Well done, Squad Six." Holmes stepped forward. "Steele, I hear you got images of the map."

Holmes might piss Marcus off sometimes, but at least the guy always got straight to the point. He was a general to the bone and always looked spit and polish. Everything about him screamed money and a fancy education, so not surprisingly, he tended to rub the troops the wrong way.

Marcus pulled the small, clear comp chip from his pocket. "We got it."

Then he spotted her.

Shit. It was always a small kick in his chest. His gaze traveled up Elle Milton's slim figure, coming to rest on a face he could stare at all day. She wasn't very tall, but that didn't matter. Something about her high cheekbones, pale-blue eyes, full lips, and rain of chocolate-brown hair...it all worked for him. Perfectly. She was beautiful, kind, and far too good to be stuck in this crappy underground maze of tunnels, dressed in hand-me-down fatigues.

She raised a slim hand. Marcus shot her a small nod.

"Hey, Ellie-girl. Gonna give me a kiss?"

Shaw passed on an iono-stretcher hovering off the ground and Marcus gritted his teeth. The tall, blond sniper with his lazy charm and Aussie drawl was popular with the ladies. Shaw flashed his killer smile at Elle.

She smiled back, her blue eyes twinkling and Marcus' gut cramped.

Then she put one hand on her hip and gave the sniper a head-to-toe look. She shook her head. "I think you get enough kisses."

Marcus released the breath he didn't realize he was holding.

"See you later, Sarge." Zeke Jackson slapped Marcus on the back and strolled past. His usually-silent twin, Gabe, was beside him. The twins, both former Coalition Army Special Forces soldiers, were deadly in the field. Marcus was damned happy to have them on his squad.

"Howdy, Princess." Claudia shot Elle a smirk as she passed.

Elle rolled her eyes. "Claudia."

Cruz, Marcus' second-in-command and best friend from their days as Coalition Marines, stepped up beside Marcus and crossed his arms over his chest. He'd already pulled some of his lightweight body armor off, and the ink on his arms was on display.

The general nodded at Cruz before looking back at Marcus. "We need Shaw back up and running ASAP. If the raptor prisoner we interrogated is correct, that map shows one of the main raptor communications hubs." There was a blaze of excitement in the usually-stoic general's voice. "It links all their operations together."

Yeah, Marcus knew it was big. Destroy the hub, send the raptor operations into disarray.

The general continued. "As soon as the tech team can break the encryption on the chip and give us a location for the raptor comms hub—" his piercing gaze leveled on Marcus "—I want your team back out there to plant the bomb."

Marcus nodded. He knew if they destroyed the raptors' communications it gave humanity a fighting chance. A chance they desperately needed.

He traded a look with Cruz. Looked like they were going out to wade through raptor gore again sooner than anticipated.

Man, he really wanted that beer.

Then Marcus' gaze landed on Elle again. He didn't keep going out there for himself, or Holmes. He went so people like Elle and the other civilian survivors had a chance. A chance to do more than simply survive.

"Shaw's wound is minor. Doc Emerson should have him good as new in an hour or so." Since the advent of the nano-meds, simple wounds could be healed in hours, rather than days and weeks. They carried a dose of the microscopic medical machines on every mission, but only for dire emergencies. The nano-meds had to be administered and monitored by professionals or they were just as likely to kill you from the inside than heal you.

General Holmes nodded. "Good."

Elle cleared her throat. "There's no telling how long it will take to break the encryption. I've been working with the tech team and even if they break it, we may not be able to translate it all. We're getting better at learning the raptor language but there are still huge amounts of it we don't yet understand."

Marcus' jaw tightened. There was always something. He knew Noah Kim—their resident genius computer specialist—and his geeks were good, but if they couldn't read the damn raptor language...

Holmes turned. "Steele, let your team have some downtime and be ready the minute Noah has anything."

"Yes, sir." As the general left, Marcus turned to Cruz. "Go get yourself a beer, Ramos."

"Don't need to tell me more than once, *amigo*. I would kill for some of my dad's tamales to go with it." Something sad flashed across a face all the women in the base mooned over, then he grimaced and a bone-deep weariness colored his words. "Need to wash the raptor off me, first." He tossed Marcus a casual salute, Elle a smile, and strode out.

Marcus frowned after his friend and absently started loosening his body armor.

Elle moved up beside him. "I can take the comp chip to Noah."

"Sure." He handed it to her. When her fingers brushed his he felt the warmth all the way through him. Hell, he had it bad. Thankfully, he still had his armor on or she'd see his cock tenting his pants.

"I'll come find you as soon as we have something." She glanced up at him. Smiled. "Are you going to rec night tonight? I hear Cruz might even play guitar for us."

The Friday-night gathering was a chance for everyone to blow off a bit of steam and drink too much homebrewed beer. And Cruz had an unreal talent with a guitar, although lately Marcus hadn't seen the man play too much.

Marcus usually made an appearance at these parties, then left early to head back to his room to study raptor movements or plan the squad's next missions. "Yeah, I'll be there."

"Great." She smiled. "I'll see you there, then." She hurried out clutching the chip.

He stared at the tunnel where she'd exited for a long while after she disappeared, and finally ripped his chest armor off. Ah, on second thought, maybe going to the rec night wasn't a great idea. Watching her pretty face and captivating smile would drive him crazy. He cursed under his breath. He really needed that cold shower.

As he left the landing pads, he reminded himself he should be thinking of the mission. Destroy the hub and kill more aliens. Rinse and repeat. Death and killing, that was about all he knew.

He breathed in and caught a faint trace of Elle's floral scent. She was clean and fresh and good. She always worried about them, always had a smile, and she was damned good at providing their comms and intel.

She was why he fought through the muck every day. So she could live and the goodness in her would survive. She deserved more than blood and death and killing.

And she sure as hell deserved more than a battled-scarred, bloodstained soldier.

Hell Squad

Marcus

Cruz

Gabe
Reed
Roth
Noah
Shaw
Holmes
Niko
Finn
Theron
Hemi
Ash
Also Available as Audiobooks!

PREVIEW - AMONG GALACTIC RUINS

MORE ACTION ROMANCE?

ACTION
ADVENTURE
TREASURE HUNTS
SEXY SCI-FI ROMANCE

When astro-archeologist and museum curator Dr. Lexa Carter discovers a secret map to a lost old Earth treasure—a priceless Fabergé egg—she's excited at the prospect of a treasure hunt to the dangerous desert planet of Zerzura. What she's not so happy about is being saddled with a bodyguard—the museum's mysterious new head of security, Damon Malik.

After many dangerous years as a galactic spy, Damon

Malik just wanted a quiet job where no one tried to kill him. Instead of easy work in a museum full of artifacts, he finds himself on a backwater planet babysitting the most infuriating woman he's ever met.

She thinks he's arrogant. He thinks she's a trouble-magnet. But among the desert sands and ruins, adventure led by a young, brash treasure hunter named Dathan Phoenix, takes a deadly turn. As it becomes clear that someone doesn't want them to find the treasure, Lexa and Damon will have to trust each other just to survive.

The Phoenix Adventures

Among Galactic Ruins
At Star's End
In the Devil's Nebula
On a Rogue Planet
Beneath a Trojan Moon
Beyond Galaxy's Edge
On a Cyborg Planet
Return to Dark Earth
On a Barbarian World
Lost in Barbarian Space
Through Uncharted Space

ALSO BY ANNA HACKETT

Treasure Hunter Security

Undiscovered

Uncharted

Unexplored

Unfathomed

Untraveled

Unmapped

Galactic Gladiators

Gladiator

Warrior

Hero

Protector

Champion

Barbarian

Also Available as Audiobooks!

Hell Squad

Marcus

Cruz

Gabe

Reed

Roth

Noah

Shaw

Holmes

Niko

Finn

Theron

Hemi

Ash

Also Available as Audiobooks!

The Anomaly Series

Time Thief

Mind Raider

Soul Stealer

Salvation

Anomaly Series Box Set

The Phoenix Adventures

Among Galactic Ruins

At Star's End

In the Devil's Nebula

On a Rogue Planet

Beneath a Trojan Moon

Beyond Galaxy's Edge

On a Cyborg Planet

Return to Dark Earth

On a Barbarian World

Lost in Barbarian Space

Through Uncharted Space

Perma Series

Winter Fusion

A Galactic Holiday

Warriors of the Wind

Tempest

Storm & Seduction

Fury & Darkness

Standalone Titles

Savage Dragon

Hunter's Surrender

One Night with the Wolf

For more information visit AnnaHackettBooks.com

ABOUT THE AUTHOR

I'm a USA Today bestselling author and I'm passionate about ***action romance***. I love stories that combine the thrill of falling in love with the excitement of action, danger and adventure. I'm a sucker for that moment when the team is walking in slow motion, shoulder-to-shoulder heading off into battle. I write about people overcoming unbeatable odds and achieving seemingly impossible goals. I like to believe it's possible for all of us to do the same.

My books are mixture of action, adventure and sexy romance and they're recommended for anyone who enjoys fast-paced stories where the boy wins the girl at the end (or sometimes the girl wins the boy!)

For release dates, action romance info, free books, and other fun stuff, sign up for the latest news here:

Website: www.annahackettbooks.com

Lightning Source UK Ltd.
Milton Keynes UK
UKHW011841060519
342194UK00001B/17/P